RUINS

A HUTCHINSON NOVELLA

General Editor: Frank Delaney

BRIAN ALDISS

•RUINS•

WITH ILLUSTRATIONS BY
SALIM PATELL

HUTCHINSON

LONDON MELBOURNE AUCKLAND JOHANNESBURG

Series Design by Craig Dodd

© Text Brian Aldiss 1987
© Illustrations Salim Patell 1987

First published in Great Britain in 1987 by
Hutchinson, an imprint of Century Hutchinson Ltd,
Brookmount House, 62–65 Chandos Place, London, WC2N 4NW

Century Hutchinson Australia Pty Ltd
PO Box 496, 16–22 Church Street, Hawthorn, Victoria 3122, Australia

Century Hutchinson Group New Zealand Limited
PO Box 40–086, Glenfield, Auckland 10, New Zealand

Century Hutchinson Group South Africa (Pty) Ltd
PO Box 337, Bergvlei, 2012 South Africa

British Library Cataloguing in Publication Data

Aldiss, Brian W.
  Ruins. – (Hutchinson novellas)
  I. Title
  823′.914[F]   PR6051.L3

ISBN 0 09 167860 9

Typeset in Monophoto Photina by
Vision Typesetting, Manchester

Printed in Great Britain by
Butler & Tanner Ltd, Frome and London

124477

'Our dreams have jurisdiction only over ourselves'
Bunny Jingadangelow

For David and Sue, with love

The Brightfount Diaries
Hothouse
The Dark Light Years
Greybeard
Cities and Stones: A Traveller's Jugoslavia
Report on Probability
The Hand-Reared Boy
The Shape of Further Things
A Soldier Erect
Frankenstein Unbound
The Malacia Tapestry
A Rude Awakening
Life in the West
Moreau's Other Island
Helliconia Spring
Helliconia Summer
Helliconia Winter
Trillion Years Spree: The History of Science Fiction

RUINS

That afternoon, they went to the movies to see Ali McGraw in *Love Story*, Ashley's movie of the moment, which was showing in Times Square. Afterwards they took tea in the Algonquin lounge since Ashley had an interest in the hotel cat. They happened to meet some old friends there, one of whom had known Hugh Billing in his musical days. They all visited a few bars, ate Mexican in the only Mexican restaurant they knew, took in some jazz on the fringes of Harlem and arrived back late at the apartment.

A cable announcing the death of Hugh's mother was awaiting him.

'Do you want me to go to Great Britain with you? I have never been in Britain,' Ashley said. 'We could take a look at London and Land's End.'

'I'd better go alone. They say you travel faster that way.'

She said nothing for a moment, contemplating him, certain he would not return. 'That's just an airline ad, isn't it? Something eats at you all the time, Hugh Billing. Your brain sure is your erogenous zone.'

'It's not that,' Hugh said, thinking maybe he should shave off his moustache or trim it just a bit. He tried to recall what London looked like.

The years had flown since Billing was last in his native country. London, seen from the taxi as he rode in from the airport, frightened him. Dirt, graffiti, crowds, miscellaneous people. Why should someone wish to write UNDERARM ODOUR KILLS on a brick wall under a flyover? He felt himself unchanged, although he was older and his moustache was trimmed. He was thin and neat of figure – an ethos of frugality, learnt from a woman in California, had ensured as much. But he could no longer think in an English way. His clothes were American, he spoke American. The shower in his London hotel wept all the night on to the cracked tiles and was cold towards him in the morning.

The years had flown. His old friends had gone from their favourite haunts. Most of those who had worked in the music business had retired or died. His sister June was dead, her widowed husband working for a shipping line in the Persian Gulf. Other people he had known had either gone abroad or had been scattered, as if a squall had blown up.

The years had flown. Only the lawyers who had sent the cable to New York were friendly, in their professional way. They gave him details of his mother's death, where the funeral was to be held, and the address of Gladys Lee, who was handling the arrangements for a small reception after the burial service. Gladys Lee was no relation of Billing's: she was his absent brother-in-law's old mother. Mrs Gladys Lee. He barely remembered her. Everyone at the reception looked strange and short of Vitamin C.

'Your mother and I weren't on too good terms, to be frank, Hugh. She was . . . not sincere. Still, live and let live.' She put a hand up to her mouth. 'In a manner of speaking, that's to say.' He couldn't get used to the English idioms. Gladys was so ancient; Billing wandered off to talk to someone else.

'I've just come back from Spain. It's a wonderful place, very orderly for a Mediterranean country. I'll say that for Franco – he does keep everything in order.' The man who was talking to

Billing across their sherry glasses was evidently of the old school, his dark suit and the aroma of moth balls it exuded being ideal for funerals. 'I hate death, don't you? Always have done.'

At the same time, he was looking Billing up and down through his horn-rimmed spectacles. He found Billing odd and Billing knew it. Only women – themselves almost always odd, Billing reflected – found him okay, accepted the fact that he fitted nowhere.

The front room of Gladys Lee's small terraced house was crowded with people who seemed puzzled by Billing. They were all old and had perfected ways of talking in patent accents. He remembered none of them. Their hearing aids were aligned against him.

The man with the horn-rimmed spectacles led Billing over to a

man mouldering in an armchair, bald of head and dull of eye, whom he introduced as his elder brother, Arthur. Arthur was scratching at his left cheek as though to check its blood-content.

'He won't be long for this world, will you, Arthur?'

'Don't let's seem to hurry him away,' Billing said, on the older brother's behalf. Wasn't Arthur allowed to make his own decision regarding mortification? Typical English, he thought. What's wrong with the country?

'Your mother liked Arthur,' said the horn-rimmed man pointedly, as if pronouncing a curse. 'Flo liked you, didn't she, Arthur?'

Arthur smiled, sighed, and returned to his cheek.

The funeral service, too, had been a disaster. The preacher had been late and either coldly inebriated or just over the safety limit of a nervous breakdown. Clasping the prayer book upside down, he had muttered furtively over grave and coffin, casting his words to the disinterested wind.

Straining his ears, Billing caught the words '. . . whom God hath joined . . . cast asunder.' The wedding service having been intoned, the mourners made their way back to Gladys Lee's place, to seek in her sherry a refuge from mortality.

'You weren't at the service?' Billing now enquired of Arthur, not long for this world.

The bald man looked up and smiled in the general direction of Billing. He raised a glass of Harvey's Bristol Cream and, drinking, spilled some of the liquid down his chin. His furry white tongue failed to reach the elusive drops where they clung to the wrinkles of his face.

'I'm excused funerals,' he said. 'Being blind, I don't see the point any more.'

Could he actually be making a joke? Billing was uncertain. He had lost his ear for English irony.

4   'You've got your sense of humour still. That's the main thing.'

He recalled that one spoke in such a way at family funerals.

Arthur nodded thoughtfully and fumbled with his chin as if it were newly discovered territory. 'I don't get as much fun out of visual gags as I used to,' he said with regret.

Seeking relief, Billing looked about for a gleam of happiness, for the sight of a pretty woman. But pretty women had been debarred from this shabby-genteel part of London. There was only old Gladys Lee in her pearls, fragile but grand, playing queen in her generally unvisited rooms.

They're so isolated, these people, Billing told himself. As I was. The Americans are much more ingenious at coping with their loneliness. Patriotism is another form of psychotherapy over there. He thought of the mountains of Utah, where he had once skied. Those wild mountains, the way American skiers dressed in bright garments to flash down their slopes like Martians, the sudden fogs which embraced Snowcat. Loneliness there had been grand opera, solitude a momentary thing with commercial value.

It was not only the English people. Gladys Lee's room and everything in it were old. No disgrace in that, or commercial value either. It was just that he had become used to new things: not so much in New York, which was to him curiously ancient, filled with old Jewish and African habits, but the great stretches of Middle America, blue-grass country, where all the furniture in all the houses had been manufactured only the year previously from extruded creamy plastic.

He excused himself from the company of the blind man and his brother and went in search of a lavatory. The toilet still had an overhead cistern and a chain with a china handle that said *Pull*. Back in time, he said to himself, as the water gurgled and frothed; I've travelled back in time. The 1973 calendar showed a picture of an old horse and cart.

Lights were on in Gladys Lee's kitchen, which was next to the john. A sturdy woman of middle age dressed in something that

5

might have been a caftan was bustling about among piles of china.

'Were you after the coffee, dear?' she called, as Billing's head appeared round the door. 'Won't be long. You can lend a hand if you like. I can't find where she's put the bloody tray. There must be one somewhere.'

He wandered into the kitchen and, in studying the arrangements, took a look at his companion. She was amply designed; brightly painted, florally scented, with a florid way of smoking, as if believing the sleeves of her dress needed to be shaken every time she removed her cigarette from her mouth. Her short hair curled into horns which lay against either cheek. Billing was pleased to see her smoke. All the career women he knew in the States did so.

'I'm Hugh Billing,' he said.

'Oh, so you're Hugh Billing.' She came forward loiteringly, having another puff and a shake. Her eyes were a dark blue and surrounded by freckles which made her, in Billing's eyes, appear intelligent. 'I'm Alice. I was looking after your mother, this last year or two. Now I'm helping Gladys out, just for today. It seems to be my role in life, so help me.'

They shook hands. As he exchanged a few words with her, Billing listened to her North Country accent, remembering it as if rediscovering a forgotten countryside. Complete with old horses and carts.

'Your mother thought the world of you,' said Alice, without a hint of reproof. 'Have you written any more of them songs of yours lately?'

'Not lately, no.'

'I liked that "Side Show". I've got a record of it at home, you know. You're younger than I thought you were, just judging by your mother's photos.'

A familiar sensation overcame Billing; like cramp, it made its presence known only when it had set in. She liked him. Fancied

6

him. She wanted a little part of him. Even as he responded by making himself agreeable, he said to himself, 'This is not for me and I am not interested. From now onwards, I want my life free of involvement.'

Hugh Billing roused the next morning to feel Alice's heavy body against his. He lay there with his eyes shut, smelling her floral perfume. Wallflower, possibly. It was a movement of hers which had wakened him.

Evidently aware that he was awake, Alice turned and put an arm round him. But it was not sex that interested her this morning. She had a number of complaints to deliver, many of them centring on her landlady, Mrs Chivers, who was making her life unnecessarily difficult.

He listened without comment. He had enjoyed being in bed with this strange and affectionate woman. Sexual excitement had made her cheerful. This morning she needed to offload her woes, her afflictions, which she did in a businesslike way. Despite her conviction to the contrary, little in what she said marked her out as special; neither in her difficulties nor her response to them was there anything that revealed in her a unique essence. Nor did she treat him as in any way individual. He was simply there to be copulated and conversed with.

Gradually he ceased to listen, trying to wonder instead about the role of fornication in modern life, as he often did. Sometimes it led to revelation, to the discovery of a unique human being. That was always a miracle. More often, it was a cover for a rejection of more complex relationships. The number of women who enjoyed sex for its own sake, as men did, seemed on the increase, he thought; they were smoking more too. It was the Pill.

There he paused. He did not want Alice. She was possessing him beyond the call of duty: Mrs Chivers was no concern of his.

7

He thought of all the women who had poured out their secrets to him over the years while he lay there, fondling them, having no secrets of his own he was prepared to offer in return.

Why was he so negative? Why had he not even a Mrs Chivers with her mean peeping-tom habits with which to respond? He was a blank sheet on which women scribbled their inner graffiti. Billing was not displeased with this striking image of himself.

He recalled his dead mother with sorrow. He had neglected her.

'Did you get on well with my mother, Alice?'

A pause.

'She liked to swank a bit, did your mother.'

Something in her voice chilled Billing.

'I must get up. I've got a lot to do,' he said, trying to think of something.

'There's a spare towel in the bathroom,' Alice said, stoical before his abruptness.

Her washing facilities were barely adequate. He recalled with regret Ashley's cosy little shower-room in her apartment in the Village. Not that he intended to go back to Ashley. He felt a kind of indifference rising in him and feared it. And he was tired of seeing *Love Story*.

As he washed, familiar music drifted to his ears. Alice was playing his old hit record 'Side Show' as she dressed.

Rinsing his face, he glanced up and saw in the mirror that she was looking round the door at him. Only her head and one shoulder appeared. In her eyes was a fixed stare. The stare did not alter when she saw Billing had noticed her. This failure of a human signal unnerved him. He stood motionless, glaring back at her in the mirror. Alice still gave no sign and simply withdrew her head after a while when the record stopped.

Billing buried his face in the towel. More than anything, he dreaded insanity. Insanity. The very word exercised a hypnotic effect on his faculties. He contrasted Alice's cheerfulness of the

night before with her dark mood, her suspicion of her landlady this morning. She had seemed normal enough, but . . . that stare . . . perhaps she was schizophrenic.

He had always feared that insanity might be catching. It was definitely time to move on.

Forty-four was an uncertain age for Billing. He recognised it as the age when men take to drink, divorce or homeopathy; but for Billing life had always contained the uncertain. His father, whom he had idolised, had died young, falling from a ladder while painting the guttering of their house. He remembered clutching his sister at the time and weeping – weeping a little more than he need have done, in order to try and impress upon her the

9

solemnity of the event. He had wanted June to care more than she had seemed to do.

He had pursued music vigorously. In music he could drown out the tragedy. As an adolescent in the fifties he got work with small bands; jazz and dance. What he liked best was trad, although, in the early sixties, a lot of other things were happening which threatened trad. Billing wrote a number of compositions of his own and managed to get solo work in various clubs. He played piano. The manager of one club advised him that he should sing, to hold the audience's attention. In something less than two hours, he wrote words to 'Side Show' – loose words, he felt, mocking, yet somehow affectionate about the world.

An agent who heard him sing and play brought Billing into a recording studio. Early in 1962, 'Side Show' became Number 1 on what was then still called the Hit Parade. Later in the year 'Count to Zero' rose to Number 2. A few months later 'Crisis' fared almost as well. Hugh Billing became part of the sixties.

'Side Show' remained in common memory and became a standard. He enjoyed no more successes, but the realisation slowly dawned that 'Side Show' was likely to pay his way through life. Provided he lived modestly, he need never work again. His manager had arranged an American Tour. He played in fifteen cities then headed for Denver where he had met a girl he liked. He never returned to England.

Or not for some years.

He married the Denver girl (she was Jewish, from Calgary in Canada) but the marriage did not last. She left Billing and was last seen heading in the direction of California with a bespectacled tax accountant. Billing returned to England for a short while and tried to write more music. But the gift, such as it was, had gone.

One miserable night, when he was without inspiration or wife, he had his recurrent dream. As usual, mysteriously, it was a week or so before he even recalled he had had it. With ordinary dreams, such things never happened.

He had been travelling endlessly down a road when two people had come to greet him and take him to their modest home. A log fire awaited him. Although the dream never allowed him to enter the house, he understood that its purpose was to comfort him.

Billing returned to his temporary job, encouraged, searching again for a magic tune.

Notes sounded in his head. He scribbled them down. But they were imitations, spurious noises, mere jangle. The words he wrote, too, were nothing but fake emotion. He could bring to them neither sincerity nor style.

Although he rejected both the music and the words, they still came to him at that time, pressing themselves on his attention, until he jotted them down merely to be rid of them. Protest as he might at this burden, he could not escape from it.

'Who was I when I had talent?' he cried aloud. 'Who was I? Was I happier then? Why do I have to write down this rubbish now? Who is transmitting this nonsense to me?'

Through the mazes of silence in his head, an answer came back. 'Wilfred Wills.'

Wilfred Wills was a hard rock group enjoying current success. The name was enigmatic and terrifying to Billing in his nervous state. It came bounding in on a strong beat at all times of day. He left a pile of three hundred and twenty unusable songs with his agent and flew back to the USA. Wilfred Wills followed, steel guitar, steel eyes, stealing his brain.

Everyone he knew in his old American haunts had gone – had taken refuge in new habits, new partners, or New Orleans. Billing decided he was in a bad way, but at least the terrible Wilfred Wills voice ceased operations during the daytime. It returned in the small hours, rumbling through his brain like an old Mack truck.

Impelled by Wilfred Wills, he began to travel.

In a Boston bar he encountered a woman quietly weeping into a daiquiri. Her name was Mary Sarkissian. She wept, she told him, not for her own problems but for those of others. She was a psychoanalyst who constantly became involved with the sorrows of her clients. Billing, signing on as a client of Mary Sarkissian, was soon involved with her.

Mary Sarkissian was a dark young woman of slight build, with delicate, braceletted wrists and a pensive expression well suited to her trade. He loved her, as he had loved almost every woman he had met since the age of six. Mary loved him and spoke eloquently of his English innocence which rendered him so vulnerable, and which she set about correcting, vigorously.

He doted on Mary, on her pensive lips, on her sad Armenian wit. He had never been more happy. The noises had gone from his head. The music was in his body and hers. He found courage enough to tell her of Wilfred Wills. She had her own little noise, she told him, a phrase from a Jefferson Airplane number she sang over and over, 'When the truth is found to be lies . . .'

'Is that aimed at me?' he asked once.

'The very question the last passenger pigeon asked.'

More bars, more daiquiris. Obliquity he could take. Besides, she smiled so mysteriously and the United States was blossoming round them. Until one day when he found Mary weeping not for their problems but for those of others. Another man with another puzzle had arrived in her outer office and her inner life.

'She liked to swank a bit.' Alice's laconic verdict on his mother, his late mother, Florence Juliet Billing, née Jones. As he collected what possessions he had and made his way back, to England and across London to the family lawyers, his mother's memory hung over him like a cloud. Over the streets and squares, cloud hung like memory.

The lawyers lived in the City. The old wartime bombsites were being built on. Everywhere was concrete, brick, glass, in stupend-ous amounts. This was not America. The scale was too pokey.

Equally, it could not be London, not the London he knew. He was floating, drifting, out of touch. The red double-decker he caught was a period-piece, bearing Billing away into regions unknown to man.

'She liked to swank a bit.' He repeated the words on the bus until they went to a kind of tune. . . . Alice had the germ of insanity in her. Perhaps the tune her words conveyed had the power to transmit that germ to others. He shivered, wondering if she had infected him. The dome of St Paul's, grey as an old oyster shell, slid between two tall glass slices of building like an immense diseased breast. He turned away in his seat, so as not to catch further glimpses of the disquieting sight.

The lawyers would disclose – or impose – his mother's will. Billing saw this as his last encounter with her unpredictable changes of mood which had so alarmed him as a boy.

'She liked to swank . . .' Mad Alice's reference to his mother's hypocrisy, to that character trait which could transform her from an otherwise loving person into a harpy. His father's early death had encouraged the trait. After coming into a little money, Florence Juliet Billing had been able to indulge her streak of pretension more freely. He recalled how sugar-sweet she would be to friends, only to fly into a rage as soon as their backs were turned, accusing them of falseness, envy, malice – all the defects from which she herself suffered. On these occasions, something in Hugh cried with terror, to fancy that she must in reality hate him too. Nothing could be trusted, no friendship could be permanent, in the face of such treachery.

He stepped from the bus and walked down London Wall, cool in the morning breeze. He saw again that vision of his father falling off the ladder. It happened for ever. The suburban garden in sunlight. He in short trousers. Running in fear. But . . . at that crucial point, at the moment when his father struck the concrete path, had little Hugh Billing been running towards the disaster,

13

or had he been running away? Memory always failed at that point. It was a source of torture. However many times he tried to recall what had happened, down came blankness, as if it were he who had died.

Dismissing his malaise, Billing continued to hum to himself. 'She liked to swank a bit – To be frank, a bit Too much . . . And so this coarse Hélène Was porcelain To touch. . . .' Then the possession of a son with successful records to his name had increased her . . . instability.

Of course, Billing's sister June, now also part of that great blank, had been odd. Perhaps her wish to set the world, including her brother, severely, pedantically to rights, had derived from a fear of her mother's pretensions. There was the early case of the biology exam question, 'Describe the function of the leg in relation to the rest of the human body.' To which young June had replied, 'The question is incorrect, since a normal human body sustains two legs.' Sustains. A nasty word. June had long sustained herself on such arid distinctions.

The lawyers, Messrs Grimsdale & Grimsdale, were friendly in their professional way, despite the fact that Billing entered their offices bearing an orange back-pack to which a miniature stars-and-stripes was sewn. They sat him at a table which had been polished every morning for eighty-five years, almost smiled and read his mother's Will to him.

He uttered a cry similar to that of a hurdler who has jumped too close to the ultimate hurdle. All his mother's money had gone to one Arthur Plumbley.

'I don't even *know* an Arthur Plumbley,' Billing mumbled, bowing his head towards the shining surface of mahogany. So she did hate me after all. Now it's proved beyond doubt. Mother – I! Your son, Hugh! Maybe she believed, or came to believe, that I jogged the ladder.

14   'Arthur Plumbley was a friend of your mother's,' offered Mr

Grimsdale Junior, in a tone of irreproachable seriousness. He had trained himself to have no gestures. The voice and the suit did it all for him. 'He is blind.' The pale hands rested.

Billing looked up. 'Arthur Plumbley? Say, was he – is he a bald guy? Furry white tongue?'

'He could be described as "a bald guy", yes.' Distasteful tone clearly implying he couldn't. 'He amused your mother in her last years.' It was a sentence Billing tried in his dismay to commit to memory. There might be a song in it.

'Shit,' said Billing. 'I met the old bastard at the funeral.' He began to laugh. Like his mother, he had his areas of insincerity. Grimsdale Junior's hands continued to rest, not unsympathetically.

Billing made his way towards Holborn Viaduct, dodging St Paul's. The pavements were broken. Old men in fur hats gathered to complain and spit in the street. He bought a pair of Scholls insoles size ten from an Indian-run chemist's shop. They had a tartan pattern. He went to a hotel to fit them into his worn shoes, then decided to have lunch there to cheer himself up.

'One must stay personally happy if possible,' he told Grimsdale Junior before leaving the lawyers' offices. 'My mother was not herself. It's dreadful for me to look back now and realise that both my mother and my father – before he died, of course – were victims of a kind of undiagnosed compulsive madness.'

Grimsdale Junior did not understand that sort of talk. He replied in a firm voice, 'The passing on of money is a serious matter, Mr Billing.'

'I was talking of the passing on of genetic material,' said Billing equally firmly, and became frightened by his own answer.

The waiters in the hotel restaurant were slack. Over curried parsnip soup, Billing watched the youngest and palest waiter   15 loading red wine into a refrigerated display counter.

'Why are you doing that?' he asked.

The palest waiter slightly altered his expression, perhaps to its fullest capacity, to indicate that he knew a daft question when he heard one.

'We just put it in here.'

'That doesn't really answer my question, does it?'

'Well, I was ordered to, like.'

'By whom?'

'The Filipinos, of course.'

Although the soup was quite good, Billing decided that neither London nor chilled red wine were for him; within twenty-four hours he was back in New York, flying stand-by. A violent shooting, with a man and a woman killed – one of them black, one white, for equality's sake – had just taken place and Manhattan was in a tense mood. Billing went to the fourteenth floor of the building off Times Square where his music agency was sited. While he was collecting the latest royalties due to him on 'Side Show', he saw an old friend of his, Neil Epoxa (born Neil Caractacus in Beirut), in the outer office. Neil had been a successful singer. Now he was an unsuccessful singer, working in a night club up on the East Side. Once Epoxa and Billing had shared confidences – about sex partners, even about earnings. Never since had Billing been so rash with his secrets.

Still, he was glad to see Epoxa. The money Epoxa was collecting from the agency made him friendly towards Billing. He was high, too, as Billing discovered.

They took a cab to a large apartment building on Riverside Drive where Epoxa was living with an older woman whom he introduced as Laxmi. Laxmi was tawny and flat-chested and wore a tawny cord suit, supported by much jewellery. She kissed Epoxa, then Billing, thrusting a neat little tongue into his mouth. It was three in the afternoon. Tongue-time already? Billing wondered; he never understood how others lived. A party appeared to be in progress. People moved about the rooms galvanising themselves into youthful postures to loud music. The furniture, a sort of cream colour, had been bought on the previous day, it seemed. It even smelt new.

'You're British, how charming,' said Laxmi, taking Billing's arm and sinking claws into it. In her other hand she clutched a toy dog, the coat of which had been dyed a flourescent purple. Laxmi appeared to have forgotten she was carrying it. 'The Britishers are so aware. My husband Norm is a Britisher. Well, in fact, he's Danish. He's around some place. Always making money. Do you do that, Heck? How was the flight? We're forever travelling around Europe. I just love the place. Ever seen the dervish house in Bukhara? I said to Norm, "Buy that" when I saw it.' She gave a laugh like the smothered bark of a toy dog.

He remembered the American habit of quoting something the speaker had previously said, as if holding it up for the listener to determine whether the remark was witty or downright stupid. He said nothing.

She showed him round the reception rooms, pointing out art objects, stepping over bodies when necessary, still clutching him tight. 'Aren't you glad to be back in the Land of the Free, Herb?'

'Hugh.'

'This picture I bet you'll recognise. The bridge at Mostar. The famous bridge. You're an aware person. I'm sure you recognise it. Hand-painted. But this next one is from Russia. It's actually painted on wood. A kind of wood. Marquetry, I believe. You can see. I did *not* like Russian food. I threw up. That's from India – the tablecloth. Norm was sick most of the time in Delhi. Then you ought to see this. It's from Armenia.'

Laxmi stood him in front of a picture with a chartreuse background, while saying in an aside to a young woman leaning against the wall, 'Betty-Ann, why don't you take a shower and freshen up, and stop screwing around with that shit cap.' Her tone had the lightness of a mother addressing a son in a dog food commercial. To Billing she said, 'It's Turkish, as I was saying. It's a straw picture and it actually depicts the estuary Turks harvesting the straw in their boats. Isn't that cute?'

'Which estuary is that?'

'I think that's what they were called. Norm is so restless. He's often planning next year's vacation before we're through this one.' She laughed, a hard dry sound like dog biscuits falling into a plastic bowl.

Billing muttered something which avoided reference to Norm's possible mental state. Neil Epoxa was nowhere in sight.

'We have some really fine Brazilian butterflies – fab, as you Britishers say – in the bedroom.' She glanced around the crowded room, but apparently saw no one to whom she wanted to speak. 'Wouldn't you like to look them over, Hen?'

He was interested to examine the flat-chestedness at first hand, so he went along. The nipples were a cheerful pink. Laxmi made passing reference to this subject just before she commenced a thorough licking operation involving all Billing's willing body, saying, 'Sometimes I wish my boobs were just slightly bigger – but Norm would probably never make it at all if they were.'

The toy dog lay on the quilted bed with them. After he had made love with Laxmi, Billing studied her husband's little bookcase by the side of the bed. *Supermarket Philosophy, Silt, Norwegian Painting: The Golden Age, Straw Pictures: An Estuarine Art, Old Slovenian Ceremonies, Nebraska in the Bronze Age.* Considering that he now had a fair picture of the absent Norm, Billing turned back to Laxmi, to find her lighting a joint. As she passed it over to him, he began to contemplate what he should do next.

The idea crossed his mind of joining the American army and fighting in Vietnam, rather as an earlier generation of men had signed up with the French Foreign Legion. A simpler way of putting distance between himself and his present life would be to hire a car and drive across the States from East to West, old-fashioned though that proposal also was.

'Shall we call some of the other guys and chicks in here?' Laxmi said, pinching out the joint.

The hired car broke down – or developed a malfunction, as the garage-hand put it – in the pleasant town of Waterloo, Iowa. The friendly young couple who ran the garage repair shop gave Billing a bed in their attic for the night. He stayed in Waterloo, Iowa, until the next spring, when the snows were gone and the wheatlands turning green from horizon to horizon. The couple with whom he became close were Ludmilla and Josef Jajack. They were of Czech origin. Their two identical old mothers were alive and dressed in gingham aprons. They ran a small market garden nearby. Ludmilla Jajack had beautiful grey eyes. She had never heard of 'Side Show'.

All the furniture in the house had been manufactured from a creamy plastic only a year previously.

'When I'm sixty, I'm going to sell everything and Ludmilla and me are going to visit Brno,' Josef told Billing, more than once. 'We've never been outside the States. When I'm sixty, we're going to ride horseback in the High Tatras. Sound good to you, Hugh?'

'Sounds good to me.'

He saw the beautiful grey eyes light up. He was sorry to leave them.

California had its compensations. It was easy to find a music job. He played trad piano in Santa Ana for a while, isolating himself from the crowd but listening to American dreams and aspirations, with which the air was thick.

'Since he left me, I've done great. I really go for business. I market yoga equipment and bean curds and health foods, do all   19 my own packaging. It's creative, you know what I mean?'

'The only money that means a thing to me is the money I make myself, right?'

'Right.'

'So I'm resilient. I have to be. I've always been the resilient kind. I never saw my mother since the age of three, except weekends in summer.'

Billings liked the look of the woman who had used the word

'resilient'. She brought to mind his Jewish wife in the marriage that had lasted such a short while. An English woman would have said 'tough'. In the word 'resilient' was stored all that rather squidgy optimism, not to mention euphemism, on which Middle America lived. He preferred it to the pessimism and the dysphemism of his own country.

When she came over to the piano for a request, he got to talk to her. She had a deep resonant voice. Her name was Robin Vandermeyer. She bought him a drink. She appeared formidable, commanding, and strode about in an outfit of suede. Even her complexion was leathery. When Billing visited her ranch-type house, he found Robin was soft and romantic inside. She showed him her doll collection. She believed that everything was going to be marvellous at short notice, despite all that experience had taught her to the contrary. It was idiotic but captivating. She decided Billing was artistic and offered him a job as a designer for a complete range of labels and promotional material.

Robin had another place up in the hills. They went riding there while Billing made up his mind whether to accept the job. In her bar that evening, drinking something pale blue, he found she had a number of Wilfred Wills records. Old fears returned. He jumped up and announced that he must go. Robin wept and threatened and snarled – all in a way that suggested she had been through this routine rather more times than she cared to tell – before driving him back into the centre of Los Angeles.

Billing soon caught the same obsession with acquiring an outdoor look as the rest of the male population. He lay about in the sun a lot. He became as brown and freckled as if he had been born that way. His moustache grew. He drank only local white wine, chewed gum and lived mainly off tuna salads. He studied the spaces of Los Angeles which, to his eye, were more astonishing than the buildings. The town was not, he decided, built for the automobile: it was built for the asocial. Its roads and freeways formed a cryptogram of isolation. He embraced the perception with pleasurable fear.

He practised looking either very friendly or very hostile. He had always had the reputation among his friends of being able to take care of himself.

But Billing was defenceless against the pale girl in the track suit whom he met in a branch of the First National Bank in Santa Barbara. She overheard his accent, accused him of being English, and then bought them both hamburgers with chillies, which they ate, knee to knee, in a crowded Spanish-type bar. She mostly laughed when she talked.

Cathy was a waif, a stray like Billing. Billing lived with her, or sometimes a friend of hers, for two years, mainly because of the short blonde hair, the fragrant little body under the track suit and her lostness. In all that time, he had no communication with England. Not so much as a postcard passed from him. The country of his birth sank below the horizon of his thought like an over-ripe moon.

Yet the moon still gleamed somewhere in memory, occasionally with brilliance. It outshone even the bright dusty Californian sun.

He sat one hot and nameless day in Choplickers, teasing a strawberry-and-passionfruit milk shake while waiting for Cathy. He was wrapped within his usual self-generated enchantment when realisation of his surroundings dawned. The little café was shrouded in darkness at midday, its low-wattage lights shielded by lead shades and aimed at the walls, as if its designer had previously worked only on war rooms. The one small window, against which Billing sat, was a blemish in its armour. With the air-conditioning, the temperature was just above freezing; yet most of the occupants wore dark glasses. Everywhere in Europe, in response to such fine weather, cafés would have spilled tables, chairs, trolleys, plants, and magisterial waiters out on to the sidewalks, in the fresh air.

Gazing through the window at the automobiles gliding by, Billing saw that they too had their windows tight closed against the heat. Like Choplickers, they were air-conditioned. In England, the car windows would be open, their drivers nonchalant, with bare elbows pointing out towards the traffic. He imagined un-American things like cyclists, pedestrians, roundabouts, horses and carts.

Oh, well, he thought, at least he had outrun Wilfred Wills. . . .

What he wanted was a close friend to whom he could describe lyrically the delights of Cathy's body, perhaps in particular the enchanting colours and contours of her buttocks; but he had never indulged in such confidences. Some elements of life remained obstinately unspoken and therefore, perhaps, un-realised; such deprivation was unfashionable on this shore of the Pacific, where telling formed a part of doing.

Inside his own air-conditioning, he was doomed to stay silent, with a quality of reticence which set him apart, even in the humble matter of Cathy's bum, not from experience itself – far from it – but from the liberation that Californians relied on experience to bring.

He decided that he was reasonably content to view his life as an ambiguous artefact, since he saw all life as enigmatic. Being lost was an adequate substitute for finding yourself. There was to be no attempt to control the flow of circumstance. Just as there was never an attempt to get anything more from the women who loved him than that which they chose to offer.

His thoughts turned yet again to his mother. Those stories of hers to which June and he, when small, had listened so inattentively. Had they been of Wales or Egypt? Had they been true? While he waited in Choplickers for the girl who might never arrive, he wished he could recall them. The stories had been memorials to good times enjoyed by his mother when young, precious to her, meaningless to her children. And now lost for ever, even if they had been – like her goodwill – largely fake.

An hour later Cathy showed up with a couple of friends. She found Billing rather silent.

She was slowly introducing him to a new way of life. She was a course-addict, she admitted, sometimes taking as many as five different courses in a week, dropping some and picking up others as casually as if Scuba, Origami and Algebra were playing cards. Billing contrasted this confusion favourably with his own apathetic state of mind in which nothing was done. Cathy had no firm beliefs, except the belief that she could better herself against the day she became a Hollywood star, although the betterment never became apparent, even to her.

At this time, all California was into space research, in an effort to better itself. Inspired, Billing decided he too would better himself. He ran his own course. It paid better.

The course – in Remedial Domesticated Space – was his own invention and the phrase had irresistible rhythm. He taught the hitherto undiscovered relationships between human beings, the synthetic environments they created and occupied and mental health. He supported his talks with multi-media presentations which grew ever more ambitious as the size of his audience increased. The word 'Remedial' was one no true Californian could resist.

'RDS is the new pace-setter for a revolutionary perception of our fair city,' announced the host of the first TV chat show on which Billing appeared, dressing in something described as a shortie caftan. 'And it has taken an Englishman to figure out the secret anatomy of our complex Californian life-style.'

Billing had a success on his hands, his first real success since 'Side Show'. He found himself working hard, engaged, making sense of the absurd proposition he had launched. He lectured at Berkeley. He became a celebrity. He wore designer track suits. He totalled his Cadillac on Interstate 5. He opened a new marina. There was excited talk of his designing a 'Star Trek' movie. Big money once more moved his way.

But Cathy held his wandering attention still, Cathy and the strange tribal drop-out society in which she lived. She remained a waif, a squatter in corners. She dreamed of grey beaches, with seals. She did not realise she had Billing. She kept hold of nothing, not even her five-year-old daughter, Pash, to whom she had inadvertently given birth. One day, Cathy lost Pash in a shopping mall; it was two days before she realised the child was missing. She would not phone the police in case her father, executive of a video company specialising in splatter movies, caught up with her. One day, on the way to a baseball game, she let go of Billing's hand in the crowd. He never saw her again.

She never even showed at the apartment they rented. Eventually her exotic fish died. Billing switched out the light over the tank, collected his things and left.

The 'Star Trek' deal fell through. A producer phoned him and wept while breaking the news. His tears sounded like they were real.

'Worse things happen,' Billing said. He meant it. He hung up. It was 1978.

He handed over the Remedial Domesticated Space course to an electronics engineer named Teddy Sly who was working with him. Sly insisted on paying him five thousand dollars for the goodwill. He also bought Billing a sumptuous volume of the paintings of Georgia O'Keeffe as a farewell gift.

Billing woke one morning in a strange bed, decided he did not care for the expression on the face of the woman sleeping beside him and once more walked out into the harsh sunlight. The road smelt of pistachio. He was disoriented. He felt sick. Hostile suburbs sprawled all about. The space ratios were distorted, expressing a general defeat which the denizens of the area did not yet realise they had suffered. Lateral expanse without elevation, Billing told himself.

He found a Mexican restaurant. It was called 'The Happy Taco'. The sign formed a dismally solitary landmark. A truck with New York licence plates stood in the parking lot. While Billing stood staring at it, the truck driver came out of the diner, smoking a cigar and scowling. Under one arm he carried a plastic two-gallon box of brandy.

'You waiting for something, Charlie?'

'Where are you heading?'

'East. What of it?'

'Mind giving me a ride?'

'Climb in. Just don't talk, is all.'

The cab of the truck was crammed with publicity photos of other trucks and of space rockets. Billing surveyed them while the man stowed his brandy away in a locker. The photos were stuck everywhere, including the roof over the driver's head, turning the confined space into a travelling scrapbook.

The driver wore a work-cap with goggles lodged on its peak, a brown leather jacket to which a sheriff's star was pinned, jeans and a pair of calf-length leather boots. He drove for many miles in silence before bursting into speech.

'Where you from, cowboy?'

'LA.' Seeing the ugly look the man shot him, Billing added, 'England originally.'

'England, huh? I heard of England right enough. The Domesday Book. I guess you think America's great, right?'

'I do, as a matter of fact.'

'"As a matter of fact". What's that mean? Let me tell you that this is the lousiest god-damned country ever lived. Full of stupid people got thrown out of other countries. Don't know nothing. I don't know nothing either: I ain't just shooting my mouth. You know how many Americans are illiterate? Take a guess, percentage-wise . . . Almost a third. Almost a third of the citizens of this great country are illiterate. Hispanics, even worse. Over fifty per cent.'

He rubbed his forehead with the palm of his hand before gesturing at the suburbs around them.

'And they all like to huddle in cities. Illiterates together. What are they afraid of?'

He fell silent.

'Are you a Marxist?'

'Hell, me? No,' said the driver. 'I believe in making money, not sharing it. It's these hippies I can't take. They don't work, they huddle in cities, screwing. Me, I go for the open air life.'

Memories of his Remedial Domesticated Space course returned to Billing. 'Then this cab is too confining for you. It conflicts with your posited character. All these pictures you have round you merely hem you in. These lorries – sorry, trucks – they put you right in the middle of a mental traffic jam.' They were leaving the suburbs now.

The driver shot Billing an innocent look. 'Is England full of cookies like you?'

Gazing out at the bleached landscape, Billing suddenly recalled the Cotswolds, orderly fields, sheep, church spires, comfortable homesteads and a steady rainfall. He longed for a taste of scones and jam, the sight of a winding road, old ladies with library books to be changed.

When they came to Waterloo, Iowa, Billing stopped off. He saw that the garden centre run by the two Jajack mothers had given place to a shopping complex. The American appetite for shopping never ceased to impress him. The complex was bigger than a cathedral. He arrived at Ludmilla and Josef's house just in time for Josef's funeral.

'He never made it to Brno. We never rode in the High Tatras,' Ludmilla said, gazing calmly at Billing from under a cute little black hat. Waterloo, Iowa, was a long way from LA and people still made concessions to mourning.

While comforting the widow, Billing was overwhelmed by a tide of love. It burst over him unexpectedly, like a spring thaw in the Arctic. It was pure, as sparkling as a stream, as fresh as happiness, as toothpaste. Never had he wanted to console anyone so much. Most of the girls he loved needed consoling.

Taking Ludmilla into his arms, Billing gazed into her beautiful tear-filled eyes and begged her to marry him. He had led an irregular life, but that was over. She was an exile, so was he; they would make a home together.

'There's a home here,' Ludmilla said, with a sob that shook her

upper parts.

He assured her they would go wherever she wished, anywhere rather than stay in Waterloo, Iowa. Even to Brno in Slovakia, if she wished. He promised he would learn Czech.

'Slovakian,' she sobbed.

Brushing the irrelevancy aside, he confessed to her how he had felt about her, how he had never forgotten her during his four years in California, how he had previously said nothing out of respect for Josef. His coincidental arrival at this time must mean something, must mean that they were intended for each other.

'But Karel . . .' she whispered. 'There's Karel. . . .'

She wept again and declared that she was happy in Waterloo, Iowa. She had never wanted to go to Brno. She had never wanted to ride in the High Tatras. She was scared of horses – and of High Tatras, come to that. All that was Josef's dream, not hers. She had been longing for years to marry Karel, Josef's handsome younger brother. He was the one scowling across the parlour at them, the muscular one, with the little finger missing from his left fist. She appreciated Billing's kindness and why didn't he take another cut of the spiced ham?

He headed for New York, to spend another two years of oblivion there, as though years were as inexhaustible as American miles. During this time, on an impulse, he sent a postcard to England, to Mrs Gladys Lee.

When he returned to the surface again, so did images of England. His money from the Remedial Domesticated Space project had all gone. New York was too world-weary to buy RDS. Billing found work around the Village until he had saved his air fare. Then he clipped his moustache, bought a cheap digital watch and returned home.

The eighties had arrived in England, despite delays. Billing himself had changed. He admitted as much to himself as he confronted gritty old London: he was thin, strange, inexperienced, in a city now as cosmopolitan as New York and almost as dangerous. Billing wore a T-shirt and spoke what passed here as American. He was neither young nor old. He surveyed the traffic with a mid-ocean eye. In this sluttish town he felt like a virgin.

Old friends had not returned to favourite haunts. His dead sister's husband was not to be found. Probably working for the Arabs. He remembered his mother's funeral, bleakly asking himself if it was because of her death that he had stayed so long abroad. In his hotel, the central heating sighed and made poltergeist noises after dark. Of remedial spaces he found none. Madness would pass unnoticed in such a place.

An older man spoke to Billing on the stairs – a surprising event in itself in an establishment where guests made themselves shadowy, withdrawing into doorways and silences to obscure the stain of their lives.

The man told Billing of a reasonable Indian restaurant nearby where one might eat cheaply.

'We could go there this evening, why not?' said Billing, on impulse.

'You're American, ain't you? I thought you was.'

There was a short cut behind a broken fence between two streets.

A path led across a waste lot where an Edwardian block of flats had been demolished and nothing built in its place. Sorrel and nettles fringed the path. It was country for two yards. Walking along it to the restaurant, Billing remembered that he had recently had his recurrent dream again, his consolation.

Together with the reassurance he felt lay a deeper, more permanent sensation, a suspicion that somehow he had allowed himself always to live cheek-by-jowl with his real life. Why this displacement? It was as if he had a doppelgänger; or, rather, as if he were merely a doppelgänger.

'What do you make of England?' the old man asked Billing, over a chicken biryani. He had a pale skin, a thick moustache and thinning hair, and the soft indefinable accent of someone born in one of London's outer suburbs. His suit was of sombre, durable tweed; it would see him out.

'I can't tell. In the USA life is so much more expansive.'

'It's getting very expensive here, too. Everything's going up. It's the government, you've no idea.'

'What I mean is – well, there's just more hope in the United States. It may be an illusion, but optimism improves – well, it improves the quality of life. You've no idea.'

He was embarrassed to think he had echoed the man's final phrase.

But his companion was not interested in the States. America for him was a dream. He was widowed and in his sixties. Suddenly, breaking a pappadom into two half-moons, he became talkative, though never eloquent. By scraps of revelation, like newspaper cuttings, he unfolded his present existence. His son and daughter-in-law had thrown him out of the room in their house he had occupied for five years. They were expecting a second child. His son had always been violent, even as a boy. He couldn't explain. His friend lived nearby; he worked down the fire station. Things were difficult. He needed to get a part-time job. Unfortunately, he had lost a suitcase full of belongings. Personal things. He had to go to Kingston. It was all chaos. Really, everything was like chaos. You had to get it together. He didn't feel he had much longer. If only he could get it all together. He planned to write a letter to his son, explaining. . . . Perhaps it would come right in the end.

'Yes,' Billing said. 'I do hope so. Look, let me pay for the meal.'

'I was a school-teacher once. One of my pupils became an airline pilot.'

Billing looked for the man next morning at breakfast, when the   *31* smiling bright Pakistani girl who served in the hotel brought the grapefruit segments to his table. The man had gone.

Billing too had his little quest. Inspired by isolation, he renewed contact with Mrs Gladys Lee, the missing brother-in-law's mother. It was the only family connection he could recall.

Gladys Lee had been old when he last saw her. She lived still at the same address. She answered the phone when he rang, voice creaking slightly, remembered his name without prompting and invited him round for a chat. He remembered 'chats'. The word came back to him from long ago. He was happy she had not said 'natter'.

'Come and chat to me, Hugh. I mean to say, not *to* me, but *with* me. . . . I'm tired of people who chat *to* me. It's one way in which people take advantage of the old.'

He appreciated her care with words, a quality with which his years in the States had made him unfamiliar. He bought a cheap suit, threw away his T-shirt and went to visit her in her unfashionable area of Shepherd's Bush. The streets seemed narrow, all forehead and no jaw.

Gladys Lee had one of the small terraced houses off Redan Wood Road, where a monastery had once stood. The area had been heavily bombed during the war; it was now rebuilt on a more modest scale. An old retired nurse with a glass eye came to wash Gladys and clean her house every morning.

Gladys Lee was eighty-eight. Her white hair was neatly set and she wore a string of pearls outside a well-cut green suit. She was frail, her flesh like an ancient beach.

'Come in, Hugh.' She made the effort of standing to greet him. She walked with a stick, bent double, and looked pained. Her pearls chattered among themselves. When seated in the tall cane-backed chair she seemed more in command and surveyed Billing with some authority.

On an impulse, he gave her his digital watch as a present. She was amazed by it.

'It was very cheap,' he said in apology.

'They saved money by leaving off the winder,' she explained.

Her living room looked out over a small damp garden, given up to ferns and green slime, to a narrow area of the street. He reconnoitred the contents of the room as if seeking out snipers; certainly, loaded as it was with unfashionable furniture and vases of dried foliage, it could provide cover for an enemy. The overall shape was indeterminate, rendered more so by the tarnished mirror over the fireplace. On the mantelpiece was lodged the postcard of the Empire State Building he had sent to Gladys over a year ago. Clearing his throat, he sat on the edge of a chaise-longue, hands clasped between his knees, and answered her questions.

He was amazed at how much the old lady found out about him within the first twenty minutes.

After that time, as though she had now heard enough, she said, 'Well, it's tea-time. Shall we have tea, or would you prefer vodka?'

'As you like, Gladys.'

'It's not as I like, Hugh. You are the guest. However, as you are kind enough to pass the decision to me, I vote we have both the tea and the vodka. Lapsang Souchong and Cossack, I'm afraid.'

Two days later, hardly knowing why, he went back to see Gladys Lee again. He chose the morning, just before eleven o'clock, when the old nurse was still fussing over her charge. Of Alice there was no sign; doubtless she was in a mental home by now. Gladys was feeling unwell; although her hands shook badly, she greeted Billing amiably enough, though with a warning: 'I'm not at my best this early in the day.'

She reclined on the chaise-longue with a rug over her legs while Billing took the cane-backed chair. The nurse served them tea and it was then, in the middle of their conversation, that Billing first heard the meretricious trumpets.

He was familiar with most bugle calls. This one he could not recognise. It sounded rather jazzy; perhaps it was of a non-military nature. Confused as to whether it was a bugle or a trumpet, he missed something the old lady said. Her skin, like the mirror above her, was speckled with brown, providing perfect camouflage.

The thin mendacious notes alarmed him, bringing to mind, for some reason, a scene in a forest clearing, where a monstrous something was being buried. He stood up in alarm. Muttering excuses, he went to the window to peer into the lachrymose street. Nothing was to be seen but pavement and brick and a selection of yesterday's cars.

'Music?' Gladys repeated. 'I hear nothing. You make me nervous, I'm afraid. Come and sit down. Why are you nervous?'

'Perhaps it comes from next door.'

'The Armstrongs do not play music at this hour of day. They're very quiet. He used to be with the Admiralty.'

After a while the music faded, was gone, was forgotten.

Billing rented a room near Covent Garden, above a veterinarian and pet shop infested with budgerigars, another English obsession. It was 1982 and already the unemployment queues were growing, but he found himself a job as porter in a supermarket. He had seen supermarkets from the administrative side in the days when his father had opened one in their home town. It soon became apparent to him that better ways of laying out the store existed, so that facilities for both staff and customers could be improved at little expense.

The manageress of the supermarket, Mrs Dwyer, was a pleasant woman of about Billing's age. She dressed brightly, was efficient, and did not bully the girls who worked at her cash-desks. Billing spent several evenings in his room, drawing and colouring plans. When they were complete, he presented them humbly to

35

Mrs Dwyer for her consideration.

'I like a man with a few brains in his head,' Mrs Dwyer said, approvingly, crossing her legs and adjusting her skirt.

The next time one of the directors of the chain was visiting, Mrs Dwyer summoned Billing into the office. As a result of their discussion, Billing was offered an office job with the parent firm. He travelled from shop to shop as an unofficial time-and-motion study man, creating new space from old. Once his work took him as far afield as Slough. He still visited Gladys Lee.

Gladys often surprised him, upsetting many of his preconceptions about the elderly. In Billing's limited experience, old people complained about the present day and told interminable stories about silly things they had done in their youth, whilst sneering about any silly things one did in one's own youth. Gladys was not at all like that.

She had done a lot of silly things, like being ship-wrecked off Madeira, getting lost in a storm in Marseilles, spending a night locked in a church in Cortina and marrying a crazy Swede. These matters she related almost incidentally; they were always subject to her clear perspective on the nature of human life, which was not so much a Christian one – Billing was surprised to find her quietly pagan – as one filled with many of the traditional Christian virtues.

She said as she poured Billing a cup of tea, 'I often dream of him,' meaning the Swede she had married. 'Though it's difficult to see people's faces in dreams, don't you find? . . . I told him when we were first married that I did not wish to live in a world in which he had no existence, yet here I still am.'

'And pretty permanent, by the looks of things,' Billings said, heartily.

'You think so?'

To break a difficult silence, he said, 'I have a dream which keeps

returning over the years.'

She vaguely indicated the bookcase behind her. 'In one of those books . . . I don't look at them as often as I used to . . . in one of them, it says that recurrent dreams are the consolation of those who have failed to reach adulthood. Is that the case with you, do you suppose?'

Suddenly he thought of Cathy, with her childlike dream of becoming a Hollywood star. Her waif-like body, the casual way he had lost her on the way to the baseball game, rose again to reproach him. Surprising himself, he said, 'I don't seem to be any good at keeping hold of love when I have it. Is that . . . that's not a failure to reach adulthood, is it?'

She never gave him any answer he might expect.

'I'm afraid your mother was a very *charming* woman,' she said. 'Don't misunderstand me, Hugh. I liked Florence. . . . I just was not sure whether she liked me. She made people unsure. Perhaps she made you unsure.'

Billing laughed. 'I know she did swank a bit. Tell me what you remember about her.'

He heard nothing to upset him. Gladys was too wise for that. He soon found that he benefited in a mysterious way from her company.

Despite this, Billing experienced guilt. He could not understand why he now shunned other company. 'Company' had once been so dear to him that he had surrendered his identity to it. Nor could he understand why he so enjoyed being with Gladys. As he sat in his room wondering, he heard again the call of the meretricious trumpets and jumped to his feet.

His left knee gave him trouble. A twinge of rheumatism, no doubt. England was so damp. Nevertheless, the tinny sound drove him into the street.

The noise vanished. Perversely, he now longed to hear it again.

It was a mild day in early autumn. The season made him think with sudden longing of his little Jewish ex-wife in Denver, so long ago. He wandered through the night. Occasionally he rested, dozing fitfully against the flanks of buildings. As it grew light, he strolled in the Notting Hill area, not far from Gladys' house, watching street markets open. He felt becalmed. He was waiting for something, something like a tune.

Wandering soon became a habit with him. Night after night, he wandered across London, listening for trumpets. Once or twice, almost daring himself to do it, he went to the terraced house where Gladys lived, sat himself down on the doorstep and dozed. Church clocks chimed, strange dreams visited him, scavenging dogs sniffed him.

He became known around the early markets. The men there called him 'Jimmy'. He often helped them to put up a stall or unload a lorry. He was invariably polite and good-natured in a mild way, as if professing scarcely to know himself. He began to neglect his daytime job.

Gladys's eighty-ninth birthday approached. He bought her a

little silver box with an embossed cherub from a stall in the Portobello Road, a huge bunch of dahlias from Kensington Park Road and a card with yachts on it from a W H Smith branch.

On the day itself, Gladys Lee wore a new costume, green tweed with a green velvet collar. The pearls were in evidence, also the digital watch. When he called at three o'clock she was feeling well, she told him, and sat with a large-print book beside her on the chaise-longue.

'We'll have a small Cossack immediately, without fooling about with the preliminaries,' she said. 'And by the way, I observe that you are neglecting yourself these days, Hugh. Your suit is very crumpled. Your shoes need a polish.'

He had not noticed. 'Sorry.'

'There are some awful people about nowadays. You should not be one of them. You are not like that. Regular haircuts are as important as regular baths.'

As he was shuffling the dahlias into vases under her instruction and manoeuvring round the obstacles in her room, he realised that her furniture had been allowed to accumulate without thought. There was a way to arrange everything which would improve her life. The chaise-longue on which Gladys habitually sat could be moved to the other side of the long window, so that she would see more sunlight outside, as well as a wider and more lively prospect.

For a moment Billing stood with the flowers in his hand. He surveyed the dresser, the many shelves, the chairs, the side tables with their freight of vases and wood carvings, the dim Impressionist paintings on the walls. He saw how it could all remain the same, while allowing the old lady easier access to the door and – if the ornate electric fire were shifted slightly – freedom from the draught of which she complained. That night, instead of roving, he worked with his pens and coloured felt tips, replanning her room.   *

Gladys Lee regarded Billing over her spectacles. 'I don't particularly wish to move a thing. It is preferable that time should not pass in this room. I have become set in my ways. For that reason, if no other, we had better execute your plan. I might even approve the result, I suppose.'

Billing gently insisted on her retiring to her bedroom whilst he carried out the rearrangements. His master touch was to bring in secretly from outside a full-length mirror which he had bought on the cheap from a dealer. He screwed the mirror to the wall just inside her living room door. As she sat gazing out of the window, Gladys would need only to turn her head to see most of her treasures, either directly or by reflection. Smiling, he went to fetch her.

Gladys professed herself delighted with everything.

'You are a wonderful and imaginative man, Hugh,' she said, touching his arm fondly.

He repeated the words to himself that night. A moon sailed overhead, flooding the streets of London with its silver dust. Just to see it in its course inexplicably lifted his spirits. He roamed as far as the Tower of London, repeating, 'Jimmy, you're a wonderful and imaginative man.' The words were like a song. Once, far in the distance, somewhere up the river, he heard the haunting bugle call, counterpointing his song.

Next evening, as he sat down facing her, Gladys said, 'You've transformed my room, Hugh, dear. I have always preserved a view of life which I cannot express in words, I'm afraid. It concerns a connection between all things in our lives. You understand my meaning?'

'My life has been very disconnected, I'm afraid.'

'I believe that the spiritual is a metaphor for the physical and, equally, that the physical is a metaphor for the spiritual. You felt compelled to transform my room and I had to accept it – as I would have done from nobody else, Hugh – because of the way you have transformed my life. Can you stay a little longer than usual this evening?'

The question alarmed him. He glanced at her brass clock and said, 'I'm a bit short of time.'

'Not so short as I.'

They regarded each other.

'There is no reason to look startled. I shall never impose on you. Even if I were tempted to do so, I should not, for fear you would disappear for ever – though in my case, for ever is not a particularly long time. What was I going to say?'

Sometimes her conversation ran off the tracks. On this occasion, with an effort, she brought it back.

'Yes, you always say your life is very disconnected. I listen to what you tell me, Hugh, dear, though you may not think so. Your life is much more connected than you know and you would be more content if you perceived its connections. Perhaps it is my duty to reveal those connections to you.'

Billing blinked a bit. 'I'm not complaining about my life, Gladys, dear.'

'Ah, well, you should, I'm afraid. You should shape your life as you shape my room. It's the only life you'll get. You don't believe in that nonsense about reincarnation, I hope, do you? In a civilised community like ours, life should be *shaped*, much as a work of art. One's hope of remaining intact lies in preserving a continuity. An artistic continuity, since you and I are not religious.'

'Life *is* continuous. Even my life.' He was pleasantly mystified.

Her book slipped to the floor. She motioned him to leave it there, lest his movement distract her.

'By continuity, I mean that we remain in touch with all the vitalising moments of various periods, dear, right back to childhood.'

He sighed. 'My childhood was rather short of vitalising

41

moments. I prefer not to think of it.'

She raised her feet slowly, bending forward in pain, and brought them slowly to rest on the damask of the chaise-longue.

'I climbed out of bed in the night, do you know. There was a beautiful moon, but I heard a fearful crash somewhere. Fearful. It sounded nearby and it continued for a long while. Like a Zeppelin crashing.

'I went out on the landing, yes, yes, the curtains really need to be dry-cleaned, and I think I went out into the street. Did I? I can't recall now, it's all so long ago, but there she was. She was smiling. It's no good arguing, I said. I saw her so clearly. . . .'

Gladys lapsed into abstraction, but after a few seconds resumed.

'There was nobody about at all. Just the moon. I wondered that everyone wasn't out in the street, just as in Stockholm, because it was such a noise. I don't mean Stockholm, I mean Madrid. What did I say Stockholm for? One of the big airliners from Heathrow had crashed on Shepherd's Bush. I could hear it – appalling.

'It caught fire and kept on and on ploughing through row after row of houses, burning like a torch. You could watch all the people jumping clear and skyscrapers falling. I've never seen anything like it before. I rang your phone number and eventually a very grumpy man answered, but he said you weren't in. He said it was four in the morning and I should go back to bed, although it was as light as day. It was a wonder the plane didn't strike this house. They come over so low, you know. Perhaps they are German. Where are they all going?'

'I hope you weren't frightened, Gladys. It was just something you imagined.' He regarded her anxiously, picturing her frail figure alone in the moonlit street, trying to place in the sky the rending noises she heard in her head. Possibly the crashing airliner was a herald of one of her 'attacks' of which she had once guardedly spoken. When the cells of the brain stem collapsed from lack of oxygen, perhaps they both sounded like, and actually

were, an air disaster, exemplifying what she had said about the
spiritual and physical being metaphors for one another.

'What was I talking about?' she asked, looking fixedly at him.
Her face took on a mask-like quality. 'What did you say about
Stockholm?' With no marked transition from her state of
confusion and without changing her tone of voice, she went on.
'As I told you, my first husband was Swedish. He was a
psychoanalyst, although he came to reject much of Freud's
teaching in view of his own experiences with his patients. I have
his books over there; you must read them some time.' She waved
her stick in the direction of her bookcase. 'I'm afraid I don't look at
them as often as I used to. . . .

'I helped him a great deal. He valued my feminine insight. Oh
yes, there is such a thing as female insight, although people make
themselves sick nowadays trying to deny it. Wearing tights, too,
is bad for female hygiene. . . .'

She looked for a long while at a picture of a horse and a peasant
beneath a tree. 'I'm afraid I'm rather tired, Alice. . . . I wanted to
ask you this: have you had any recurring dreams throughout
your life? Perhaps you would bring me a glass of water.'

Distressed, Billing hurried to the kitchen to fetch her a drink.
The kitchen was the room in which he had first met the Alice
whom Gladys's words accidentally conjured up.

He held the glass to Gladys's lips. Her livid hooks of hands
closed over his, shaking the glass until the water splashed her
dress.

'What can I do? Call the doctor?'

'That man will do me no good. No, leave, Hugh, leave. I hate
being ill. Even more, I hate you to see me ill. Leave. Come
tomorrow, come tomorrow and I'll be better. Come tomorrow
and we'll talk about dreams. You will come?'

'He kissed her cheek. 'Bless you, Gladys, dear. Of course I'll
come.'

Billing took a bus back to his digs. Mrs Dwyer was waiting for him, standing about the hall in her fawn coat, clutching a fawn handbag under one arm. His heart jumped.

'I need a drink, Rose,' he said. 'I'm a bit upset. Come round the corner to the pub and let me buy you a drink. How are you? Lovely to see you.'

As they settled companionably at the bar, Mrs Dwyer said, 'I was just going home. I've been hanging about here for an hour. I must be daft.' She lit a cigarette from a gold lighter, looking him in the eye meanwhile.

'My husband will be furious when I get home, want to know where I've been, what I've been up to and so on and so forth and all about it. I thought we were meant to be liberated, but not me, no.' She laughed, a curt vexed action which pinched her face.

'I'm sorry to keep you, Rose, I've been seeing an old friend. What's the trouble?' Even as he asked, he knew. He had not been to work for three days. He had simply forgotten.

It was none of Mrs Dwyer's business, she said, messing about with an ashtray, and they scarcely saw anything of each other any longer, but she had been at head office and had happened to hear Mr Motts Senior say that he would be forced to sack Hugh Billing if he did not pull his socks up.

Billing clutched Rose Dwyer's hand on the stained wood of the bar. It was a firm, dry hand, its nails painted carmine.

'You're good to me. Thanks for warning me.'

'I'm fond of you, Hugh. You know that, I suppose. Why do I say such things? What's your problem?'

'Have you got a woman or something? Your suit's all creased.'

He looked anxiously round the lounge bar, searching the faces of the other drinkers. 'What's that tune they're playing? It must be very popular nowadays. I'm always hearing it.'

'I don't hear any tune,' she said flatly. 'No juke box here. Only that Space Invaders contraption.'

44   'Haven't they got tapes or something playing? It can't be in my

head. Bugles or trumpets – I can't quite tell which. Is it Herb Alpert?'

She looked impatiently at him, pursing her lips. 'Stop changing the subject. If it's not women, what is your problem?'

Shaking his head, he withdrew his hand. 'It's no good asking me, Rose. Somehow the bottom fell out of my life. You know I was a – what they call a drop-out in the States.'

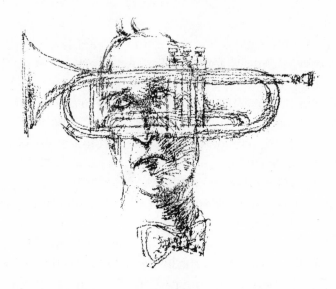

'Well, you're back in bloody England now, mate. You want to be yourself. Hang on to what you've got and be thankful.' She clutched the fawn handbag, illustrating her point by instinct.

He looked down at the beer stains. 'But who am I? I lack continuity. . . . I don't know, Rose. Work's not important to me.'

'What is?' she asked him sharply. Then, when he did not reply, repeated, 'What is important to you, then?'

She puffed her cigarette, watching him not unkindly.

He drank his drink and looked across the bar. 'I never have any luck. With women, for instance – I seem to lose them all. They never stay. Nothing's permanent. That's the hallmark of my existence. Nothing solid to show, just ruins.'

'Don't talk so silly, man. You're lucky to have women at all. . . . Besides, ruins *are* permanent. That sort of attitude will get you nowhere. Strike a light, Hugh, I don't have to spell it out, but if I wasn't married to Harry, I'd move in on you and try to set you to rights a bit, really I would.'

He laughed with sad pleasure. 'I could do with a bit of that, that's certain. How about trying anyway?'

Sighing, she said with a wistfulness unusual in her, 'What a little lost lamb you are. . . .'

She drained her glass. 'I must get off home. Look at the time. Now, mind you turn up for work tomorrow and don't say I didn't warn you.'

'Rose, dear, you're lovely. London's full of people and not a one like you.'

'Just as well. Bloody fool that I am.' She blew him a kiss as she went through the door.

He sat for a while over his empty glass before leaving. Rose's cigarette stub smouldered in the ashtray beside him. He returned to his room. Drawing the curtains, he opened the cupboard where he stored biscuits and marmalade on one shelf and brought out his drawing materials from the lower shelf. Then he settled down at the table, shoulders hunched in concentration above the cartridge paper.

After work next day, he took his drawings round to Gladys. She had given him a key to her front door. As he let himself in, he wondered apprehensively if the time would come when he walked in and found her dead. Serve him right for making an insensitive remark about her looking permanent. Perhaps his little ex-wife was dead too, somewhere across the ocean.

But no, Gladys was as usual in her living room, standing with the aid of her stick, peering out of the window. He went over and kissed her furry cheek. She vibrated slightly.

'I've brought you something to look at. It's silly. I'm all right on plans but I can't draw for toffee.' Another English phrase.

He spread his pictures out on the floor as she settled herself slowly in her accustomed position on the chaise-longue.

'How are you feeling today, Gladys?'

'I'm all right,' she said, constrainedly, looking down at what he had drawn. She spent so long looking at the pictures that he started to apologise all over again. Gladys cut him short.

'Don't run yourself down, dear. They're rather good. They'd be better if you had proper artistic materials. The colours in fibretips are too garish, too what I call chemical. Think how lovely this church would look if you had a real stone tint, eh? Not that black.'

'They call it grey on the lid. I tried to sketch phases of my recurring dream for you. You asked or I wouldn't have bothered. My one recurring dream.'

Billing sat on the carpet by her feet and explained his dream. Pleasure filled him as he spoke. He suspected Gladys was lapsing into the insanity of the aged, but the thought did not alarm him.

He would have been no more than four when the dream first visited him, he said. Thereafter, it returned from time to time. He could not say how often. He could not say when the dream last visited him; not since he had returned from the United States, from Iowa, from New York, from wherever he imagined he had been.

In the dream, he was walking down a long country lane, weary and lost. Sometimes, details of the journey remained clear. Sometimes, he saw stones beneath his feet. In later versions of the dream he saw hedges covered in dust, dying foliage. On one occasion, he passed burnt-out cottages. Once, dead cattle. The countryside was always calm and deserted.

He was approaching a church, standing on a slight rise ahead, an old stone-built church with a square tower, in the Early English style. Dusk was falling. It was always near sunset in his dream. The ground was obscure with mysterious movements. *47*

His sense of isolation increased when two figures, dark against the westerly sky, moved from a place of concealment. They stood in the middle of the tawny road, awaiting his approach. Both wore old-fashioned clothes. One was male, one female; the woman wore a poke bonnet and a stiff black bombazine dress, while, in the earlier versions of the dream, the man wore a high silk hat. They were rigidly immobile, not moving till he was close.

They were waiting to greet him. Their hostility was a mere figment of his anxiety, his lostness. They were smiling at him. Nobody, certainly no strangers, had ever been so glad to see him. They took him by the hand and escorted him from the road to the rear of the church.

The grand-looking church, he was surprised to find, was in truth nothing more than a ruin, a half-demolished shell, its interior blackened by fire. This he could see clearly, for this interior was lit by the setting sun. He paused, looking askance at the man, who smiled and indicated that he should proceed.

A flat area like a stage had been cleared in front of the ruin. Some of it was paved in tile. Another building had been constructed inside the shell of the old church, a much humbler structure, a mere cottage. Here the two old people lived, and they were welcoming him into their home.

Stones from the church formed the walls of the building. Indeed, a part of the old church served as the rear wall of the cottage. Its roof was thatched, its windows leaded with diamond panes. It lay within the embrace of the grander structure.

As the old couple shepherded him forward, he realised how beautiful the cottage was, and humble. The rays of the sun, which was about to sink below the distant skyline, lit the window panes brightly. The front door swung open. Inside gleamed a log fire. He heard the crackle of flames. The two old people gestured courteously to him. The dream always ended before he could enter.

*

'And how old were you, do you say, when you first had this vision, dear?' Gladys asked, after a silence.

Striving to answer, Billing looked down at the sketches on the floor. He had drawn one version as a Victorian sentimental picture. A second sketch was more austere, with the church tower fading in a ghostly way into the evening sky. To a third he had given a wartime emphasis; the building in the background had been ruined by shellfire, while the figure that represented his lost self was in uniform, complete with steel helmet and rifle.

'I must have been four the first time. I sat on my mother's knee

to tell her all about it. And before my sixth birthday . . . that was when my dear Dad fell off the ladder and killed himself. . . .'

Scarcely were the words out when Billing began weeping as he had not wept for countless years and the tears splashed down on to his sketches. His whole frame shook with sobbing. Horrified as he was by his performance, he could not staunch the tears, had no idea from what deep well they came. He felt Gladys's frail arm round his shoulders, but still the grief went on, like a river pouring from a glacier.

At one point he heard himself say, 'You see how my life's in ruins – without a father I never had any . . . any pattern of approval. Even women could not give me a . . . give me a permanent . . .'

The sobbing swept away his words.

Later, he was mopping his face, childlike, and apologising.

'You poor dear,' Gladys said, 'you were robbed, robbed. Life can be very cruel. And your mother can't have been a great help. As we've agreed, she was a bit of a . . . bit of a swank. . . .'

She mopped her eyes but her general calm in the face of these earth-moving revelations was reassuring.

So ashamed was Billing of his weakness in revealing his emotions that he did not go near Gladys Lee's house for several days. By night, he roved far afield, through parks and stone streets, walking with echoes and shadows. He had learnt how to travel on the underground without paying. From the underground, he transferred to an ordinary train, and travelled down to Winchester. He slept that night against the door of the cathedral, but the season was growing cold. The rheumatism returned, bolder than before.

He got back to London. His firm had sent on to his digs his employment cards and a small payment owing; Mr Motts Senior had finally acted.

It was the weekend. Escape was the only thing: he would return to California. Living was easier there. He might take up RDS again, make a movie, find a new woman. All he need do was earn the air fare. He pocketed the last of his money and went on a rare drinking bout across town, in Hammersmith, home of some market porters he knew.

'Jimmy, Jimmy, stop your running!' someone called to him as

he was heading towards Gladys's house after midnight. He ran in earnest then, making Shepherd's Bush echo to his footsteps, looking back to call derisively at the man, looking ahead again just in time to see the great black lorry bearing down on him, like a shark on a drowning baby.

Dr Platt was young and smart and carried himself very straight. He smelt chemically clean. He had a small moustache and was sharp in a friendly way with the patients in the surgical ward. Billing recalled, with a feeling he did not analyse, the time when he had looked like that. Dr Platt's suit was impervious to creases in the wrong places.

'You can leave hospital tomorrow,' Dr Platt told him. 'You're lucky, old chap. It's a simple break and all you'll need is a crutch for a while. The abrasions on your trunk are healing well. Of course, that arm may take longer. You're not as young as you were. What are you, fifty? You'll survive.'

As he was walking on, Billing called to him, 'Doctor, excuse me – do the nurses have to play that music all the time?'

'Radio One? I don't care for it myself, but most people like it, or get used to it.'

'No, I mean at night, when the radio's off. Is it a tape they play? That everlasting bugle, or whatever it is.'

Dr Platt shook his head. 'I don't follow you. There's nothing else. You're hearing things.' He walked away, paused, sighed, then returned to Billing's side.

'Perhaps you *are* hearing things, old man. How long have you been conscious of this music?'

'Oh . . .' He was confused by the unexpected question, did not know what to say and was afraid of losing the doctor's attention. 'I couldn't say. . . . Some while.'

'What's your theory?'

'What theory?'

The doctor tapped a ball-point pen against his thumb nail. 'How do you account for the noise? Most sufferers have a theory about the noises they hear. Flying saucers. The Russians. The CIA. The chap next door. A secret ray. I just wondered what your theory was.'

'I thought it was the radio. I don't have any theories. You mean it's in my head?'

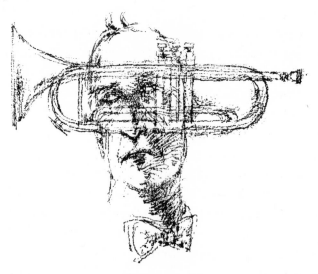

'The noise is called tinnitus. Many older people suffer from it. Nothing we can do about it though some recommend a change of diet. Don't worry.' He gave a smart nod and passed on to the next patient.

'What did he call it?' Billing asked himself. It would be nice to be a member of the professional class, as his father had been; to walk away briskly after making a statement, not to have life hanging round you like a question mark. One day, Dr Platt would age and hear noises in his head, too. But not for a long time. . . .

It was strange to be outside again, and even stranger to walk with the metal crutch. He did not dislike the feeling of importance it gave him. He must *do* something with his life. In particular, he would go and see Gladys Lee.

It was afternoon. He sat in a coffee shop in Knightsbridge not far from the hospital, lacking courage. He talked to the other customers, beckoning them over for a chat, until the manageress came up and asked him courteously to leave. At a second café, the manager spoke less politely. He limped into the park and lay by the Serpentine, watching people go by, hoping to see someone he knew.

His thoughts turned to his mother. She had played a mean trick, leaving her money to that blind idiot. Perhaps he had really hurt her by being afraid of her. After all, what if she was a hypocrite and liar? What if she did swank a bit?

Why had he been incapable of loving her, bereft as she was of a husband? He might then have freed both of them. With her death, that chance had passed away.

The discomfort of his thoughts drove him from the park. Outside a cinema, a woman's face gazed down from a hoarding. Her eyes were smiling perhaps a little vaguely, the expression was calm, bereft of passion. 'Night Music' was the name of the film. Smaller letters said, 'And Introducing Kathy Cleaver'. Billing stood mute, staring up into her eyes. It was his Cathy. Maybe her dream was coming true. Certainly she was not looking at him.

Early next morning, Billing reached Gladys's front door and sank down on the step. He dared not unlock the door and go in. She would still be asleep, drugged by the pills she took. He slept himself and was roused two hours later when the old nurse arrived.

'Why, you'll catch your death of cold, Mr Billing, sat there like that. Fancy! You'd better come in and I'll make you a hot cup of tea.' The glass eye seemed to gleam with compassion.

He stood up stiffly, aware of his injuries, his age. His suit was crumpled. It was true that he felt chilled, yet he entered the house reluctantly, afraid to confront Gladys in case she was angry with him.

For the first time, he noticed the unpleasant closed smell of the place.

The unusual time of day made everything in the house revelatory. As the nurse disappeared into the kitchen, he paused undecided on the threshold of Gladys's bedroom. It was a room he had never been invited to enter. He looked round uncertainly, examining the landing wallpaper, which exhibited, from floor to picture rail, a faded pattern of stags attacked by wolves. Morning light filled the house with mist and shadows. He entered her room.

She was in bed. He had never seen her so early, just awakened, looking so much more in the clutches of death than usual. An evil smell pervaded her bedroom. She panted unpleasantly, as if she were an old dog, peering at him from the sheets through rheumy eyes, displaying broken pegs of teeth.

'Go away,' she said.

He waited miserably in the living room, clutching himself inside his damp clothes, resting his crutch against the cane-backed chair. 'Sorry,' he said aloud.

On one of the side-tables lay a parcel which, on inspection, proved to be addressed to him. He recognised Rose Dwyer's handwriting. She had sent on a few items from his rooms. There was no note in the parcel. So he was homeless as well as jobless. He could say nothing when the nurse brought him in tea and toast spread with melting peanut butter.

An hour later, Gladys Lee hobbled slowly into the room with her stick. Billing stood up, nodding his head to denote affability. After shooting him an angry look, she turned her gaze elsewhere. Her pearls rattled.

'I didn't expect ever to see you again.' Her tone was flat, unsmiling, her head sunk between her shoulders.

He smiled feebly. 'I've had an accident, Gladys. I gave your name to the hospital as my next-of-kin.'

She went and sat by the electric fire, hunched over her stick, staring into the glowing element, not speaking for a long while.

'You look a mess. . . . What day is it?'

Billing remained standing, propped on his crutch. He said, awkwardly, 'I'm glad to see you again.'

'You still haven't had your hair cut.' She gestured with a blotched hand for him to sit down.

'This dream of yours – why did it comfort you?' She came straight to whatever her point was; she had no time to waste.

'It always brought me comfort. . . . That is to say, I mean. . .' He tried to live with young people because explanations were always due to the old. 'Each time the dream comes, it has a new significance. It enfolds my life.'

The old lady sat where she was, still staring into the fire. The nurse brought her a tray of breakfast, consisting of half a grapefruit, two thin slices of toast, coffee and pills, which Gladys regarded without apparent recognition.

'Go into my bedroom, Hugh. Look at the framed engraving hanging on the wall on the far side of my bed.'

Billing did as he was told. The nurse had thrown back the covers of Gladys's bed and opened the windows to air the room. The curtains billowed inwards. He held a curtain back with one hand in order to study the picture Gladys had designated.

The engraving showed a grand ruin. Ferns and small trees were growing over it, so that it resembled a man-made cliff. The original structure, long in disrepair, had patently been intended for reverential purposes: its proportions, its grand arched windows, indicated as much. Centuries and wars had caused its original function to be lost, and its fabric to be largely destroyed. From the fallen masonry, a modest house had been constructed. It stood within the embrace of the old building. From its windows

55

washing hung and people in the costume of the period stood outside it, idly enjoying the sunshine.

It was a perfect realisation of his dream. He stood transfixed by it, by its grandeur, which he contrasted with his own crude sketches. With a flash of perception – what was it but a flash that visited him, like lightning in a summer night? – he saw that neither building held much interest alone, the ruin or the house. Only in their juxtaposition was there piquancy, a cause for speculation.

As he stood in front of the engraving, he had a godlike view of himself from above, standing before the spectacle of the world. His pains, his losses, were encompassed within the greater panorama of his existence. Even the memories of his parents, his dear lost wife, were less than the love they had shared.

'It's one of Piranesi's Views of Rome,' Gladys said, bent double in the doorway. 'Perhaps you can read the inscription underneath. I was never good at languages. The grand old building was the mausoleum of Helen, mother of Constantine.'

The names meant nothing to him. He said – without turning round, without removing his eyes from the picture – 'Death – a mausoleum. Yes. So with me, a walking bit of antiquity. My makeshift life built within that larger shadow. My flimsy walls the debris of past generations.'

He was aware of the effort she made to speak.

'That applies to biology in general. Not just to you, or to architecture. . . . Our general inheritance. . . .'

Not seeing exactly what Gladys meant, he said bitterly, 'Every day of my life would have been different, better, more productive, if my father had lived.'

Yet while the words were leaving his lips, he perceived that, as he interpreted the engraving, so must he interpret his life. If his

interpretation of the engraving was not forged by all he had lived through it would be nothing more than a meaningless pattern. His existence had design, meaning, piquancy, even to himself, because of the relationship between the sorrows which over-shadowed the past and the understanding granted in living moments. The glimpse of unity made him whole. He clung to it as he clung to the crutch.

'Hugh.' She drew near and rested her yellowed paper hand on his sleeve, either for need of balance or affection. 'I have always valued that print. It was my husband's. I've never been to Rome. . . . No, not Rome. Someone said something. I liked Stockholm. . . . To me it represents the processes of the mind, the inheritance the new draws from the old, through many gener-ations. Imagine how astonished I was when your sketches recreated virtually the same picture. . . .'

She gasped with pain and turned slowly back to the door while still speaking. Her frame shook. She rattled the doorknob furiously when she held it for support.

'When you wept, I wept too. Something communicated with us. . . . Many people regard this engraving as a gloomy thing. Not I. Far from it. Well, it has shown us its vitality. Through it something communicated with us.'

For him, the transitory trumpets were playing.

When he did not respond, the old woman paused on the landing. 'This is the occasion for a very early application of vodka, my dear. We can celebrate – nurse, nurse! Where is that bloody old woman?'

Later, when they were in the living room, Billing in the cane-backed chair with his crutch on the floor beside him, Gladys seated on the chaise-longue and the bottle and ice and glasses between them, he stared at the pattern on the carpet and said, 'Pictures and dreams – how can they make any difference to the facts of life?'

'Facts are open to interpretation, just as the picture is. It's not the picture that's important but its interpretation. . . . Pictures and dreams. No, you removed the chest when we went to live in Malmö. My silk stockings were in that chest. It's pure carelessness. . . . What was that? No. What was I saying?'

He sighed. 'I don't know. About interpretation. I'm out of a job, I know that. Nowhere to go, life in ruins.'

'Yes, of course. Everything with any meaning has many meanings. The picture preserves a meaning for us jointly. You see, I am the old ruin, Hugh, and you are the new building. You must come and live . . . within my walls. Before I fade out. . . . There are two rooms upstairs never used. You can throw out a lot of the rubbish. All rubbish. You can be at home here. I shall try not to be a burden to you. I know I'm a burden. You need not see me every day, even. We could make it a rule of the house. Only every other day and then only for so long. An hour, two . . .'

He regarded her old and lined face, her trembling white hair, the hands that rested, one in her lap, one on the curved back of the chaise-longue.

'I'd have to be free to come and go, Gladys.'

She sighed deeply and coughed. Pursing her mouth until the lower part of her face was a maze of wrinkles, she asked, 'Is that your only response, to evade responsibility?'

'I don't want mothering.'

She gave a dry laugh. 'That kind of untruth is another evasion, dear. What's certain is that in my last years I do not require a baby son to look after. Perhaps my offer was a mistake, too generous. I'm weak in the head, that I know, I'm afraid.'

Billing went down on his good knee beside her and clutched the skeletal hand in her lap.

'Take me in,' he said. 'Please take me in. I'll just have to be free to come and go, that's all. There's a woman I must see again.'

The lane was long. In his dream he seemed to have been walking for ever. He did not recognise the curiously distorted trees that grew on either side of the way.

Yet the ruin ahead was familiar. It had been an ecclesiastical building in time gone by and now bore a crown of grass and ferns growing from the remains of the roof and the broken window-sockets. The evening sunlight bathed it in a ruddy glow.

Two people stood in the middle of the road, waiting for him. He felt hostility in the air, before realising that it was his hostility towards them.

The strangers escorted him round to the back of the ruin. There, in contrast to the general decay, stood a modest dwelling built from fallen masonry. He recognised that he was in exotic country; yet the occasion held a haunting sense of home-coming.

Washing hung in a small courtyard, strung between old and new walls. They walked under its damp folds in order to enter by the front door, which stood invitingly open. The elderly couple moved aside to allow him to go in first, their hands extended in a gesture of welcome.

He hesitated for a moment, looking round uncertainly, seeing for the first time how wild the country was all about. The setting sun filled it with mist and shadows. He turned. This time he entered the dwelling.

RESTORATIONS

'I shall never be able to look back on the funeral with any pleasure,' Rose said, gloomily. 'This just about ruins the day.'

She had been standing beside the car, the poor defunct car, with her arms akimbo; now she climbed into the back seat and closed the door firmly, not slamming it but shutting it loudly enough to express a finite but not negligible amount of disgust.

Billing made no answer. He stood where he was, hands in pockets in front of the car, regarding the scenery.

The stretch of road was deserted, apart from an occasional lorry growling by. They were stuck somewhere north of London. No building was in sight. Trees lined the road, with fields beyond. They were waiting on the northbound side of the road, in a lay-by into which they had pushed the Austin. Tall trees, firs and ruinous pines a century old, formed themselves up into untidy woodland beside them. It was almost dark. Minute by minute the air thickened.

The breakdown people should arrive at any time. Hugh did not permit himself to say the words, knowing that he had spoken the sentence aloud before. It would only annoy further the woman he wanted to console. But the garage was being a long while coming. He had had to walk three miles to a phone box to summon them.

He made an effort now to stay in touch with Rose, strolling over to her window and saying, in firmly cheerful tones, 'I'm sorry, I'm no good at dealing with car engines. I expect it's the armature again.'

Rose remained looking down. 'I know, Hugh. You're the dreamer.' She had flattened all nuances from the remark, so that only the words remained, spiritless between them.

Billing turned his back, resuming a contemplation of the roadside copse. It was a chilly February day and the sun had already set behind the trees. While the man and woman waited by the car, the hectic colours of day's end had died from the sky. Now only muted tones remained: shades of oyster, lemon, pearl and then, nearer the horizon, a series of greys and tones neither grey nor blue. The rough trunks of the trees presented themselves in silhouette against this backdrop, providing an avenue towards the distance.

It seemed to Billing that from this arrangement of colours and space something spoke to him, addressed him gravely yet comfortingly. He felt an answer arising in himself. Outwardly he was mute, his usual unkempt self contained within the dark suit he had bought especially for Gladys Lee's funeral.

He thought, I'm a funny fellow. I wonder if Rose feels all the sensations I do? He was too shy to ask her directly, suspecting that the answer could be deduced – the answer he had found throughout life, that no one felt things as he did. Of course, old Gladys had done, no denying that. But she had become quite gaga towards the end.

It grew darker yet. He watched the great drama through the trees as if it would never happen again. Rose climbed out of the car and begged him to get in, in tones the over-strained patience of which suggested a mother's tact with a wayward child.

'I bet it's the armature. And the fan belt,' he said.

They sat in the back seat, holding hands.

Darkness had closed in definitively when headlights appeared and a vehicle pulled into the lay-by. Billing jumped out and went over to the cab.

'Watson's garage?'

'I'm Watson.' The driver was a nondescript man in overalls with a mass of uncombed hair, his plain face made more shapeless by the cigar wedged into one corner of his mouth.

'That smells like a good cigar,' said Billing.

'It's a Fischer Florett, mate. You can't buy them in this country. I buy a supply of them when I go on holidays in Switzerland.'

'It makes a change to see a man smoking a good cigar nowadays.'

'What's the problem with your vehicle?' As Watson spoke, he emerged from his cab. He was a disappointingly small person, his round head hardly coming up to Billing's chest. Without waiting for an answer to his question, he stomped off to look at the car for himself.

Rose had emerged from the rear of the Austin and said hello to Watson.

'You two been to a funeral, then?' he asked, opening up the bonnet, again without waiting for an answer. Rose went over to Billing and took his arm. They stood helplessly while Watson shone his torch and peered about in the engine, muttering as he did so.

'It's the armature, I think,' Billing told him.

Watson eventually slammed down the bonnet and went back to his truck. 'Major trouble, mate. Didn't you never have that thing serviced? It's leaking oil from every joint and your cylinders have seized.'

He operated a series of levers on the side of his truck. A hook descended, which he secured under the Austin. He then hitched the car up until only its back wheels remained on the ground.

'Better climb in the cab with me,' he said. ''Less you want to stay here all night.'

They squeezed in the front beside him and had the benefit of   63 the Fischer Florett all the way back to the garage, which stood on a bleak crossroads at the edge of a village.

It was late when they reached home in a hired car.

'What a way to finish up a funeral!' Rose exclaimed, as she made them some tea.

'It turned out better for us than for Gladys,' Billing said, grinning.

Prodding the teabags, Rose said, 'Fancy the car breaking down. And two hundred pounds' worth of repairs. I hope that man Watkins is honest.'

'At least we didn't come to any harm. Watson.'

'Watson or whatever. Hugh, I think you enjoy breakdowns, I think your whole life is broken down.'

He was humble with her because she had really remade his life; but then he was humble with everyone.

'I've never achieved smartness, like you. My physique wasn't made for it. I admire the way you dress, Rose. Don't let me drag you down to my standards.'

She kissed him as she handed over his mug of tea. 'Must Do Better. Where are we going to find a spare couple of hundred pounds? We've still got to pay for this carpet.'

'Something will turn up.'

'I could cheerfully kill you, sometimes.'

He was already on his way next morning to the garden centre where he worked when the post arrived. It consisted in one letter only. Rose opened it. The letter came from a solicitor in Islington, announcing that the late Mrs Gladys Lee had left all her estate to Hugh Frederick Billing.

It was five years since Hugh Billing had first met Rose in the London supermarket where she worked. She left her husband when she discovered through a friend that he was having an affair with a woman in the next street.

'The very next street!' she kept exclaiming. Billing wondered if she would have forgiven George Dwyer had the other woman lived three streets away; but he held his peace and discovered to his delight that she was prepared to live with him. Which she did without fuss.

'I'm a decent working-class woman and I don't expect a fat lot, Hugh,' she told him. 'A bit of courtesy and kindness and I'm yours.'

He remembered how courteous she always was with the girls in the supermarket. Together they looked for somewhere to live. Rose wanted to escape from London and George and eventually they found a rented flat in a side street in St Albans. He was perfectly happy in an expanding garden centre just outside town, while she worked as supervisor in a supermarket in Watford. Every Saturday he caught a bus in to London to go and see Gladys and spend the afternoon with her.

In that way he had witnessed the old lady's gradual physical deterioration. Her nature remained much as ever, calm and slightly inclined to give orders; she was always pleased to see him, and Rose too, when Rose appeared. Rose, at first inclined to resent this usurper of Hugh's free afternoons, also grew fond of the old lady and took her boxes of Rose's Chocolates from the supermarket.

'Without doing much, I am good for her,' Billing used to say. 'As her doctor heals her, so do I. It's the company, the attention. We all need it.'

'So you keep telling me,' Rose said. She had been born in Manchester, but her parents had come to London when she was eleven.

'But you see it's been good for me, Rose, being good for   65 someone else. We've each got benefit from the friendship.' It had crossed his mind once or twice that there might be more rewards for him when she was gone; he dismissed the thought as avaricious and distasteful.

Gladys's mental deterioration, when it came, was sudden and unremitting. She saw her room filling up with snow. Soon there were men of snow closing in on her armchair, men who would not or could not speak to her. Gladys whispered about these things from a stricken face which looked as if it was even then isolated in the middle of a terminal blizzard. After she was discovered wandering in the streets in her nightdress they took her to hospital. There most things were white and she died of it, after a screaming fit.

'Wandering, just as I've spent my life wandering,' Billing said with a shiver. But he was anchored at last, anchored by Rose, by the flat, by the fact that he now wore clothes she chose for him, by the fact that they were saving up for a bungalow of their own, that they had rented a TV set, that she cared for him enough to seek out a suitable diet so that the bugles no longer shrilled in his head, calling him away.

It was part of his new rootedness that he took to reading while Rose was sitting in front of the TV watching quiz games. From a second-hand bookseller in town he bought the longest and heaviest novels he could find: *The Apes of God, Confessions of Felix Krull, The Good Companions, Anthony Adverse, Don Quixote* – Billing read them indiscriminately, knowing nothing of their standing in the world. Later he graduated to non-fiction, reading with the same lack of discrimination he had once shown in other fields of endeavour.

Both he and Rose felt they were educating themselves. The neighbours were nice people but talked only about the garden and home wine-making.

Their wine itself was passable. Rose particularly liked the

turnip and tea wine. Billing stuck to the potato, which he christened 'Spirits of Spud'.

His wandering had ceased. The phantom bugles were silenced. His dream of that long journey down the lane had not recurred for – Billing could not recall how long. He ascribed its absence to the way in which the Piranesi engraving had brought both dream and contents to the light of consciousness.

When Billing and Rose drove to London again in her old Austin, repaired at great expense, to claim the house in Shepherd's Bush which was now theirs, he at once took her upstairs to look at the engraving in Gladys's bedroom. Rose was not greatly impressed.

'Gloomy, isn't it?'

She turned and flung open the window, then leaned out and regarded the cat-traversed gardens below.

'Do you think you'd be happy here, Rose?' Billing asked her broad back.

'You've got to be tough. Be thankful for what you can get.' She straightened and closed the window with a few thumps. 'Sash cord's gone. Shepherd's Bush is a nice area. We'll have to clear out all Gladys's junk . . . Yes, it's fine. I mean to say, like, beggars can't be choosers.'

He liked her grudging ways, knowing the kind heart beneath. True, there were times when, harking back in memory to his days in the USA, he regretted that she had achieved Zero Life Style. Americans of even a non-affluent layer of society always achieved a Plus Life Style in some extraordinary way. Like Italians.

Rose had a collection of china horses – he had contributed one himself, a shiny coltish thing with brittle legs. But it could not be said that she was *into* china horses, as an American would have been. It remained simply a collective hazard on the mantelpiece, a somewhat forlorn reminder of a lost Rosey past which had contained fields and pastureage and idle summer afternoons.

So he put his arms round her, coat and all, and kissed her.

'Don't really mind where we live,' she said, kissing him slowly, 'as long as you keep slipping it up me.'

'Oh, god,' he groaned. 'Don't worry your pretty head about that.'

Downstairs, in the main room, he contemplated the chaise-longue.

'We'll have to get rid of that, for a start, Hugh . . . I like this long mirror, though.'

'Nice, isn't it?' He looked in a drawer. Among the clutter of items he saw a birthday card with yachts on. He stared at the bookcase, pulling out the odd book, hoping for something to read.

'We'll have to get shot of that lot,' Rose said behind him, indicating the orderly spines.

'Not so fast. It's nice to have books about.'

Some were in foreign languages: German, Swedish. There were several books bound in drab green and written by a man named Bengtsholm. Looking at an inscription in ink on the title page of one of them, he realised that Bengtsholm was Gladys's husband. After his death, she had reverted to the use of her simple maiden name of Lee, Bengtsholm presenting too many obstacles to the insular English. Many of the books in the case had been his, or were actually written by him. Billing felt awed and excited.

He opened one called 'Of Analytical Psychology' and read, 'Something must be left to your own mental efforts. You might consider what it means to be complete. People should not be deprived of the joy of discovering themselves. To be complete is a great thing. To talk of it is entertaining, but is no substitute for being it. Being complete, however you phrase it, is the main thing in life.'

He stuffed the book back, recoiling. In his mind was an image of that ladder falling and the body going with it. Complete? Psychology filled him with dread – yet it was a pleasurable dread.

There were mysterious doors and possibilities, as he knew.

The Psyche and Dream Journeyings. Why not just *Journeys?* The title caught his eye as he was about to turn away. *The Psyche and Dream Journeyings* . . . He pulled it out. It was another great long unexplored volume, with clear print, thick paper, heavy binding and plenty of footnotes.

'We'll have to do something about the kitchen,' Rose called. 'I should reckon this here oven sailed with Noah on the Ark.'

They went out the back into the damp little garden, in which Gladys Lee had not walked for many months before her death. Most of it was down to grass. An old iron bath stood at the far end, under the grey slate-capped wall. Buddleias grew. There was a rockery covered with ferns. On the whole the soil seemed too poor to sustain weeds.

'We could do better with this,' Billing said, airily indicating the landscape. 'Conifers at cost. A figure or two. Trellis. Clematis.'

'Get old Frewin down here to help us,' she said. Frewin was the name of their wine-making neighbours. They had a good laugh about that.

By the kitchen window was a dilapidated shed containing nothing but a broom and old linoleum. Unwanted things could be stored there and eventually they could have a car-boot sale with them.

They looked up at the slate roof, the peeling windows (bathroom window frosted half-way up), rusty gutters, wrinkled brickwork.

'It's ours!' they said proudly, and hugged each other. 'All ours! Wonderful!'

'If we sell everything, it'll bring us in enough cash to completely redecorate inside,' she said. 'George taught me how to hang wallpaper. I'm a dab hand at it. We'll make it look all lovely and light and modern inside and banish Gladys's ghost. Oh, it will be grand! Better than Buckingham Palace.'

'I'll paint the outside. We'll need to get a long ladder.' Inwardly, he was a bit sorry about banishing Gladys's ghost. In some odd way, he longed to preserve everything as it was, in all the seedy pomp of yesterday; but he said nothing, recognising that ultimately Rose's practicality would triumph over his nostalgia. Probably quite right, too, he said to himself.

Staring at the rockery, he ceased to listen to what she was saying concerning the hanging of wallpaper. A woodlouse was climbing up the slope between two shoulders of stone. A miniature avalanche of soil sent it slipping to the bottom of the slope but, undeterred, it tried again and eventually disappeared behind a brown frond of fern. One snowdrop was flowering in a hollow beside a boulder of clinker.

Weeks passed. Billing and his lady hugged themselves frequently as the realisation of their fortune sank in. It seemed as if they could never discuss it enough. To have a house of their own gave them security and, more than security, dreams.

Rose rearranged her week so that she could take Saturdays off as he did. On Friday nights, they'd drive away to London in the Austin, taking with them such food as jam tarts, pork pies, cakes, and taramasalata, to spend all weekend in Shepherd's Bush, refurbishing the house, picnicking, chatting, calling to one another.

At the far end of the garden, by the old bath, Billing made a bonfire of various tatty pieces of carpeting while Rose scrubbed the floors of the house with disinfectant. Billing turned off the water supply at the mains and extracted an ancient cast-iron hot water tank from the cupboard next to the kitchen, replacing it with a more effective copper cylinder plumbed into what had been the kitchen broom-cupboard. The cupboard that was now empty he painted with emulsion paint and filled with shelves; so they acquired a pantry. A good secondhand refrigerator fitted neatly into it. Another hug was required when that was in place, and much self-congratulation.

Asleep in the double bed with Rose that night, Billing had a bad dream.

He and Rose lived in a great house which seemed to fill a whole countryside. The corridors went up hill and down dale like mountain paths. They were happy until a stern personage in grey and white uniform came to separate him from her. Doors slammed, mysterious winds blew.

He was taken to a confusing garden, flowerless and a muddle of small constructions. At the far end of it stood a little rundown building, guarded by wooden fences and gates. The personage led him into the building, saying that henceforth Billing had to live here.

It seemed that the building had once been a poultry-house. Although Billing did not wish to enter, the personage would brook no protests. It was a low one-storey place. The doors were stuck and opened only with difficulty, creaking as they did so.

The interior was worse than could be imagined. All was in tones of grey. The frosted windows were clouded with cobwebs. Mould and dust covered everything. The atmosphere was dense and fusty, while the floor appeared to be paved with decaying cheese. Billing found he could scarcely walk.

The personage (now very faint) said, 'It will not be too bad.' It then faded away and Billing was alone, shut in.

His feeling was one of intense grief. He wandered about without any fixed intention or plan of escape. Worse was to come. He found himself in an interior room, more distressing than the others, more suffocating.

The room was ill-lit. Amid dark shadows, propped in one corner, sat Gladys Lee. She was shrouded in dust sheets and sunk in her final demented stage, her eyes red-rimmed. She beckoned

71

Billing forward. Her mouth fell open with a terrible crack, revealing broken sticks of teeth.

Billing woke feeling sick and sat up in bed. The crack still rang in his head. He was convinced it was real.

Leaving Rose to sleep, he made his way barefoot downstairs. The staircase was presently uncarpeted. By the light from a streetlamp he saw that the glass in the front door had been shattered. Retreating, he went back to the top of the stairs and switched on the hall light.

A half-brick lay on the mat inside the door, with fragments of glass all round.

He went and woke Rose. 'What time is it?'

'It's only half-past twelve. Who'd do such a thing, do you think?'

She pulled a face. 'Bloody Dwyer, who else? My husband – George Dwyer, the drunken cretin. Him and that bird of his from the next street. He must have seen us coming and going round here. I wouldn't put anything past him.'

They went down and stared at the damage. Hugh found a piece of cardboard with which to block up the hole, while Rose swept up the fragments of glass and had another swear.

'It wouldn't have been your George,' he said, squatting down beside her. 'No man would do a thing like that deliberately. It must have been a passing yob, hitting our door by accident.'

'You don't know George. Friday and Saturday nights especially, when he's had a few.'

'But how would he know where you were?'

'Oh, he'd find out. Don't forget he's a taxi driver. He's got friends crawling all round town, he has. One of them must have seen us in the street, unloading the car or sommink.'

When they had cleared away all the glass, they had a cup of tea
before returning to bed. Going up the stairs, feet cautious of

splinters on the rough treads, he suddenly said, 'Friday and Saturday nights . . . You mean he might come back tomorrow night?'

'Oh, I suppose he might. He can be a vindictive little bugger, can George.'

'I must say you take this pretty calmly.'

'Hasn't nothing of the sort never happened to you when you were in the United States? Are the Yanks all that different? You picked up enough women there, by all accounts.'

The double negative irritated him. 'Is that how the working class goes on? Bashing up property?'

'We certainly don't make a little tin god of it, like you posh fellers.'

He burst out laughing, partly in annoyance. 'Oh, forget it. Let's get to bloody sleep.'

Saturday evening saw Hugh Billing in a nervous state. It was dusk when he finished giving the side door and window an undercoat and swept the side passage with the worm-eaten old broom from Gladys's shed.

'We'll have to do something about Dwyer,' he called in to Rose, who was working in the bathroom. 'Otherwise, we'll always be worrying.'

He kept his real worry to himself. Dwyer had become a vast figure of evil in his mind. Not knowing what the man looked like, he was free to imagine an ogre, bent on the destruction of their happiness. Dwyer was a nightmare, linked to the nightmare from which the smashing of the glass had roused Billing. He was a spectre beyond reason, which had to be laid. The thought of him brought Billing to a state close to paralysis. But he fought against his nerves and, with Rose's none too reluctant help, developed a plan, based on the premise that Dwyer, to have thrown a brick with any accuracy through the front door, would have had to stop his cab temporarily opposite the house.

On Saturday nights, they generally went down to the local pub for a drink and a bite to eat. On this evening, they had supper 'at home', as they already began to think of it. By ten o'clock, the remains of cold smoked herring, salad, and Jacob's Club biscuits were cleared away and they sat staring at each other.

'He may not show up, of course.'

'Seems a bit unlikely.'

'Yes.'

'Still, he might.'

'I know. Be prepared, eh?'

'It's always best. Teach him a lesson.'

'A bloody good lesson.'

'Else we'd never feel safe.'

'I'll go outside.'

'It's far too early.'

'Better be ready, just in case.'

'You're right there.'

By ten-thirty, he was in position in the front garden, concealed from the road by a wispy privet bush. The nearby street-lamp lit the front of the house. Billing and Rose had planned everything carefully. They had pinned a sheet of cardboard over the unbroken pane of the door and left the door standing open. Billing had even gone to the trouble of crumpling up a few pages of the Daily Mirror, placing them where they could be seen, on the upper step and in front of the open door. In the darkness, the house thus presented a derelict air, attractive to the vandalous-minded. Rose waited inside while Billing crouched uncomfortably by his bush. He felt the gravel under his thin shoes. A twig scratched persistently at his right cheek. One buttock nudged the railings which marked the extent of his property. His right hand was cold where he clutched a poker, his offensive weapon, too tightly.

What a mass of contradictions you are, he told himself. You're in acute fear of this Dwyer, you see him as an ultimate brute. At the same time you long to get at him, to kill him, even. Rose is to blame for all this. How did I get into such a mess?

More deeply, he thought, Father didn't care one bit for me or he would never have allowed himself to fall off that ladder. Such things are never really accidental. If he were still alive, he'd give me some guidance and protection in life and not let me drift. Now I'm going to get beaten up, all because of him.

He clutched the poker tighter.

By eleven, he had stopped thinking.

Some people went past in the street, most of them quietly. Cars roared by, including the odd taxi. A dog came and barked tentatively before moving on. The air grew colder.

By eleven-thirty, Billing had had enough. He whistled to Rose and went inside.

'We mustn't give up,' Rose told him, giving him a hug. 'This is about George's time. Have a snort of gin and then let's get back on watch again.'

'I've had enough.'

'Just till quarter past twelve. We must nail the old bugger if we can.'

Back by the privet, Billing immured himself to hardship by recalling scenes from his American past. Taking over a new apartment in Riverside, hearing a phone ring as he entered and running from room to room trying to locate it. Being in a woman's house when the mosquito door banged and in came a businesslike dog with a cigar in its mouth. The woman – her name had gone – taught rehabilitative drama at the Alabama State Penitentiary, Children's Division. Waking in Greenwich Village and finding that someone had built a punk tree outside his window, made entirely of copies of the *St. Petersburg Times*. A sign on a road outside Atlanta, Georgia, erected in sorrow or pride, saying 'One driver in every ten on this road is drunk'. America was much more surreal than England. It was a pity.

His wandering thoughts were recalled by the sound of a car stopping on the far side of the street. He crouched lower, glancing at his watch. It was ten minutes past midnight. A man was getting out of the driving seat of a cab. It was Dwyer! This was it!

Everything was still. The orange London smog sulked overhead. The man walked slowly across the deserted street, hands in pockets.

Billing gripped the poker, fear gripped Billing.

The man came slowly to the iron gate. He stood there on the pavement, scrutinising the front of the house, with its half-open door, its lightless windows. He was a small, thick-set man, rather less terrifying than Billing's imaginings. He wore a bomber jacket and cord trousers.

Suddenly he moved, looking to left and right and then, finding the street empty, running forward, covering the front path in two strides and reaching the steps that led up to the open door.

Billing jumped from concealment without thought, brandishing the poker. At almost the same time, Rose emerged from the shadows with a bucket of cold water, which she flung at Dwyer. Unfortunately, Billing, in his excitement, had given a shout of challenge as he emerged. Dwyer turned, fists ready.

Some of the water hit its target. Quite as much soaked Billing.

He struck out boldly, blindly, and the poker caught Dwyer across one shoulder, thwacking into the bomber jacket.

Cursing, Dwyer started to feel in one of his pockets, kicking out at Billing at the same time with a toecap to his right calf. Billing dropped the poker and punched Dwyer on the jaw. Dwyer responded with a left-handed punch which struck Billing full face. Blood immediately poured from his nose. His sight became foggy.

Another man jumped from the taxi and came across the street, shouting, intent on supporting Dwyer.

Still swearing, Dwyer managed to pull a knuckleduster out of his dripping pocket.

This was too much for Billing. He ran round the side of the house to the back garden, Dwyer in pursuit. Both men were shouting.

Rose hurled her bucket at the second invader. She ran down, seized the fallen poker and brandished it. The second man retreated respectfully and went to stand on the far side of the taxi, evidently deciding not to face an armed woman.

Billing almost fell over the broom he had been using earlier. Dashing blood from his face, he grasped it, swung it, and caught Dwyer amidships. With a grunt, Dwyer seized the free end of the broom. Then commenced a kind of folk-dance across the back lawn, each combatant fighting for possession of the weapon. Dwyer did a good deal of cursing. Billing gritted his teeth and hung on. He had an idea.

With the house between the fighters and the streetlamps, it was dark in the small back garden. He was at an advantage; he knew where things were. He had realised that, for all his aggressiveness, the taxi driver was a foot shorter than he. This was not an invincible enemy. The thought gave him hope. He set to work to manoeuvre Dwyer where he wanted him.

It did not take long. Dwyer stopped shouting and started to pant. The waltz they were doing became slower, the turns more gradual, even the supply of swear words more halting.

'You leave my bloody missus alone – we got no quarrel between us,' Dwyer said.

'She'll never come back to you.'

'I rescued her from a life of drudgery.'

'She hates your guts.'

'You should have met her father.'

'She hates your guts, Dwyer!'

And there they were. Putting all his strength into it, Billing charged. With the business end of the brush in Dwyer's chest, he was forced to run backwards. There were only three or four steps to go. The next moment the back of his legs struck the curve of the side of the old bath.

He gave a cry and fell in backwards, helpless to save himself.

The bath was full of dark and oily rainwater, under which all kinds of unnameable things lurked. Among those things Dwyer was momentarily to be numbered. He surfaced, spitting and retching. Billing pushed him under again with the head of the broom.

'I'm – help, I'm drowning!' cried Dwyer, gasping. Billing pushed him under a third time, enjoying it. He thought he could actually drown the man and who would know? It would make the world a better place.

'Swear you'll stay out of our way and never bother Rose again,' he shouted, when Dwyer next surfaced. He kept up the pressure with the broom against Dwyer's chest.

'Yes, yes, I swear. Let me out of this filthy muck.' He spat a leaf out.

'Swear!' Prod, thrust.

'Yes, yes, I did swear. I do. No more, guv, help me!'

Billing stood alertly by with his trusty weapon and allowed Dwyer to climb out of the bath and flop on his hands and knees. Dwyer pulled himself up to head blindly for the entrance, hands out before him. All fight had left him.

'And never come bloody back,' Billing shouted, as the defeated foe climbed damply into his vehicle and drove away with his friend. The taxi vanished round the corner of the street.

'You're marvellous, Hughie,' Rose said, embracing him. 'You settled his hash. Come on in and let me mop your poor dear nose.'

'I fixed him,' Billing said, proudly letting his nose stream. 'I sure fixed him good.' John Wayne couldn't have managed better.

'Your poor nose.' She put a hand on his arm.

'Don't bug me, woman,' he said.

Then he caught hold of her hand and went indoors with her, rather shakily, dripping blood.

Back in St. Albans, Billing went to the doctor and got a certificate to remain a week off work. Not only was his nose grotesquely swollen; two crescent moons of a troubled crimson appeared to underline his eyes. It was a time to lurk away from the sight of men and, more particularly, from inquisitive small boys.

Nothing could injure his morale. He had fought and won. Now at last he would have a home he could legitimately call his own – its integrity gained in combat, as it were. He had at last found a native hearth and a surcease from wandering. His old recurrent dream had fulfilled itself; he was at last allowed home to his own fireside.

Yet his spirit, he told himself, was not entirely at rest. As he interpreted the dream, it was his parents who should have admitted him to the lesser home within the greater. He did not see the dreadful Dwyer as standing *in loco parentis*; that had been Gladys's role.

These thoughts no more than ruffled the surface of his sea of calm. Yet they recurred when he sat in the old armchair during a week when he might have been working and instead sailed steadily on through the deep waters of the tome entitled *The Psyche and Dream Journeyings*.

In its pages, he encountered people with all kinds of strange misapprehensions, living distorted lives. 'Thank heavens I'm not like them,' he said to himself, marvelling. He read of a woman who could not distinguish her husband from other men, a man who could make love only when clutching a baby pig and other extraordinary cases. He wondered what those cases would have done with their lives if they had not suffered from their disabilities. It soothed him to think how lucky he and Rose were to be normal.

Before they returned to Shepherd's Bush the next weekend, they gave notice of the move to the landlord of their flat. Their new house was now fit to live in.

It was late when they arrived in Shepherd's Bush on the Friday night. Walking through the fresh new rooms together, still smelling appetisingly of paint, they decided to go to bed at once so as to make an early start in the morning, laying vinyl flooring in the spare bedroom and finishing the tiling of the bathroom.

Before turning in, Billing took a stroll alone in the garden. He wished to see the old bath which had played such a vital part in his victory over Dwyer. The black water which half-filled the receptacle lay still, without a ripple. It reflected the moon, full that evening and shining overhead, sublimely free of the rooftops and chimney pots.

His heart seemed to open as he gazed up at it. Not just a dead world but a symbol trailing its mythic connotations across the sky. Beautiful, inspiring. He recalled some of the strange associations the doomed people in his book had conjured up: the moon, for instance, as a female spirit, as the Anima in men's minds.

The book of dream journeyings made mention of the baboons at the great temple of Borabadur who perform a gesture of adoration when the moon rises. All savages fear the dark, some believing the day to be God's creation and the night the product of the devil, of Satan. So the moon is a heavenly promise. Its crescent is symbolic allusion to the power of the feminine principle. 'Diana, huntress, chaste and fair . . .' There is a timeless quality about her, suggesting wisdom. When the Anima is encountered in dream wanderings, it is like a visitation from the moon among the thickets of the night; and then the Anima often manifests herself as a young woman, to offer guidance or temptation. Her appearance is frequently a sign that a period of confusion and trouble – the night journeying of the psyche – will give way to the daylight of individuation. Anima dreams can be memorably vivid, lingering on in retrospect as tokens of hope long after other dreams have faded with break of day. All this and more, for the books on Gladys's shelves were ample in discussion. Billing hardly knew whether or not to believe them, but the fact was that he wished to do so, for obscure reasons, and so he remained entertained if not convinced.

As he walked by the bath with these and similar thoughts in his mind, his gaze on the sky, the moon, at the extreme end of his walk before he turned about, appeared to become entangled in the bare branches of an ash tree.

So greatly did this sight move Billing that he stumbled back inside the house, as if he could bear no more loveliness.

He thought of that loveliness again after he and Rose had made love, after he turned the light off and darkness filled their little room. In his present complacent state, he realised, he had had no dreams he remembered for some while. Nothing, except the nightmare provoked by George Dwyer's flung brick. It was as though the moon had not shone on his sleep.

The pale moonlight was already at their window panes. Humbling himself, Billing carefully formed words like a prayer in

his mind: 'Oh, Anima, I believe in you. Visit me, speak to me, in my dreams tonight, fair creature.'

On waking, he knew the Anima was alive in his mind, almost as tangible as Rose's head on the adjacent pillow. She was there, leaving only as his eyes opened. She spoke to him.

What she said was: '*Your parents loved you all along.*'

Billing rose in a daze and went into the bathroom. He stared at himself in the mirror, feeling his face. Letting water run into the bath, he went and sat in it naked. He sighed, shook his head, marvelled.

It was the truth. Something had responded to his entreaties. He never doubted for one moment that she – fickle though she might be – had visited him, had spoken – and of course had spoken truth. Undeniable Anima, undeniable truth.

Lying back in the water gasping, he clasped the soap like a heart to his chest. Yes, yes, she had spoken! He was in communication with himself. The psyche had made a true dream journeying and returned from it with treasure. His parents loved him.

His father loved him. All these years, the ghost of his father, of that falling ladder, had not been laid. In his childish mind, he had seen himself as either the subject or the object of the accident, as responsible for it, or as purposely injured by it. He had held the belief that his father died to punish him. Somehow the poisonous error had always lodged within him like a wound.

Of course that was nonsense. His father loved him. His Anima declared it.

Again the ladder was falling. Again he heard his father's hoarse cry for help. Then the smash of ladder and body against the concrete walk. He was running towards the smash, crying for his father not to be hurt. His father made no reply – his father who loved him.

It was all clear. He could recall it all for the first time. The fearful blankness had gone.

And his mother came running, pushing him away in her fright, clasping his father's body.

He remembered it all. The weeping that followed. Weeks of weeping. His helplessness. His guilt. The funeral to which his mother thought it best not to allow him to go. His boyish agony over that: as if he had been turned away from the very grave. And all the time she and his father had loved him. Their dear son, their dear only son.

The joy could no longer be withstood. With a great shout, he jumped out of the bath and rushed into the bedroom, naked and dripping, to the sleeping Rose.

'A miracle, a miracle!' he shouted. 'Rose, wake up.'

She sat up and threw back the bedclothes.

'Come in,' she said 'you daft bugger.'